PC
L50

BIG TROUBLE BY THE DAWN'S EARLY LIGHT

The sun rose brilliant into the wet air, a tremendous burning orb, riveting in its demand for attention. And John Slocum reached for his Remington, and fast.

For they were there, without the slightest warning other than the feeling Slocum had in his guts. A wave of screaming Indians riding up and out of a hidden draw with the sun at their backs burning into the eyes of the startled cattlemen. It was as though they had erupted right out of the ground.

D1715619

OTHER BOOKS BY JAKE LOGAN

JAKE LOGAN

TEXAS TRAIL DRIVE

BERKLEY BOOKS, NEW YORK

TEXAS TRAIL DRIVE

A Berkley Book/published by arrangement with
the author

PRINTING HISTORY
Berkley edition/May 1990

All rights reserved.
Copyright © 1990 by The Berkley Publishing Group.
This book may not be reproduced in whole or in part, by
mimeograph or any other means, without permission.
For information address: The Berkley Publishing Group,
200 Madison Avenue, New York, New York 10016.

ISBN: 0-425-12098-8

A BERKLEY BOOK ® TM 757,375
Berkley Books are published by The Berkley Publishing Group,
200 Madison Avenue, New York, New York 10016.
The name "BERKLEY" and the "B" logo
are trademarks belonging to Berkley Publishing Corporation.

PRINTED IN THE UNITED STATES OF AMERICA

10 9 8 7 6 5 4 3 2 1

1

Plain as the wart on the end of the fat dealer's nose, John Slocum saw it was time to get out of town. Town was Fort Worth, Texas; the scene was Jolly Burns's High Time Saloon in the section of town known as Hell's Half Acre. The gaming room had fallen suddenly silent as the man named Rudabaugh, the man with the big red, shiny hands, called John Slocum on his straight flush, which topped Rudabaugh's full house.

"There ain't that much luck in the whole of Texas, mister. Slocum, ain't it? Slocum from Georgia, I heard. You get me, Georgia boy? There ain't that much luck in the whole of anywheres!"

Slocum did not like being called "Georgia boy," especially in that tone of voice, especially by the bigmouth sitting across from him. But Link Rudabaugh was well boozed, and he didn't catch even one of the warning looks that went around the table and among the onlookers of the game. He was ready to kill. And said so.

"You better go for it, you sonofabitch!" And his hand struck fast as a whip to a hideout in his shirt as the members of the poker game dove for cover.

But Slocum was faster. His own hand licked out and smashed Rudabaugh's wrist against the edge of the hard table, causing him to cry out in surprise and pain. The next thing the man knew he was on the floor, tangled in his chair, with the big round card table on top of him.

"Get up," Slocum said, hard, his right hand near his Colt. And he stood back a little, giving Rudabaugh room.

"I got nothin' against you, Slocum," Rudabaugh said as he got to his feet. "I just don't like losin', see." And he spread his sore hand, a look of pained innocence on his face.

But Slocum wasn't fooled. And in the next second he was proved right, for Rudabaugh's hand swept again toward his gun—this time the one at his hip.

Again Slocum was faster. As Rudabaugh came up with his Colt, Slocum had cross-drawn his own weapon and fired, shooting the gun out of his hand. The man screamed and charged, a raging bull.

Slocum stepped easily aside, tripping Rudabaugh with his outstretched foot, then smashing him along the temple with his fist. Link Rudabaugh fell like a poleaxed steer. He lay on his back, his gun hand numb, his nose bloodied, and the side of his head already turning into a nasty dark red-black-and-blue.

In the silence that fell a man belched softly. The room was otherwise frozen.

Then the batwing doors opened and a man with a tin star on his shirt strode in.

"What happened?" He stood looking down at the man who was still out of it. "Holy Mother of God! Link Rudabaugh! Never thought I'd see the day!"

The marshal was a lean man with a long nose, and he gave every impression to John Slocum and the rest of the room that he knew his business. His name was Bill Shine.

"What happened?" he said again, looking around at the silent faces.

"Man here didn't take to bein' called 'Georgia boy,' Marshal." This neutral comment came from an older man with white whiskers and a longhorn mustache. He was wearing a dusty black Stetson hat plumb center on his shaggy head.

"Real observant of you, Doc," the marshal said dryly. "You do this?" he said, cutting his eye to Slocum.

"He tripped over my foot," Slocum said easily. "After he called me on my straight flush."

"Where's Burns?" Marshal Bill Shine's hard eyes swept the gathering. "And you men get back to what you were doing."

"I'm right here, Bill." A dumpy man with a grainy voice and bright red galluses stepped through the parting crowd. "And what this here stranger says is true, more or less. Rudabaugh was lookin' for trouble. I'm billing him for a new table, and for interrupting money which, but for his shenanigans, could of been comin' in over the table and bar."

"Where you stayin', stranger?" Marshal Shine asked. "And I already heard your name on my way in."

"Chip House," Slocum said, looking down at Rudabaugh, who was starting to stir.

"You have sure put your foot up your ass, mister. Of all the ones to give a going over, you picked a sweetheart. That is one of somebody's important men, I do believe. 'Ceptin' I ain't mentioning a name." The marshal suddenly reached up and started to pick his nose. "On second thought, you better come on down to the office with me, Slocum. I have heard of you-all, and I aim to check up on some of my flyers."

"I'm not wanted anywhere, Marshal," Slocum said.

"Exceptin' right here," Shine said. "I be wanting you." He canted his head down at the still prone Rudabaugh, who had lifted his hand to his face, as though to feel whether or not his nose and mouth were still there.

"Some of you boys help him. Carry him outta here," the marshal said.

Jolly Burns took the center of the room. "Morgan, you and Tersh there get this mess cleaned up. You fellers can get back to your cards now." He clapped his hands together. "C'mon now. Get this man outta here."

And as Slocum and the marshal of Fort Worth started out of the saloon, an old-timer with a broken nose, a wheeze, and the stink of booze and chewing tobacco on his breath stood looking down at the man on the floor, who was still on his back, only just beginning to try to move.

"Big bastard, ain't he? Looks like you fellers gonna need a cant hook maybe to turn him over." And he cackled with glee at the thought of turning the fallen gladiator over with a logging hook.

• • •

After visiting the marshal, Slocum didn't go back to Jolly Burns's saloon but decided to pick a different place for refreshment. The Elkhorn appeared likely, and while a few heads looked up as Slocum moved to the bar, the attention was casual, and he felt he could melt a little more easily into the crowd than at the High Time, where he had beaten Link Rudabaugh.

He stood at the end of the bar, nursing a whiskey and enjoying a Havana, glad for the moment to think and decide on what he was going to do.

Actually, he had already decided it was time to leave Fort Worth, especially when the marshal informed him again that the man he had beaten was one of the town's vigilantes.

He had asked Shine why there were vigilantes about when he, as marshal, was obviously the law, and also obviously doing a decent job.

Shine's reply had been succinct. "I'm getting the notion that maybe I been too good for the boys."

Slocum had turned that one over for a moment, being careful how he replied. "Looks to me like you're maybe in the middle of something, Marshal."

Bill Shine inclined his head, squinting against the smoke from his cigarette, which he'd just built and lighted. "Maybe," he said. And Slocum could see the lawman was giving no ground. Anyway, the situation in Fort Worth didn't look good for a man such as himself, especially after backwatering a key figure like Rudabaugh.

"You mind yourself, Slocum," Shine had said then. "If I was in your boots I'd be heading out of town. I mean like right now."

"You advising or telling?" Slocum asked.

"Both." And Bill Shine had stood there looking right at the big, broad-shouldered man with the thick raven-black hair, the cat-green eyes, and the grace of movement of a wild animal. He was thinking how glad he was not to have been in Link Rudabaugh's shoes. He was glad, too, that there was nothing official against Slocum that he would have to enforce as a lawman. Slocum was clearly not the type who would take kindly to such an occasion. Though Bill Shine was a man who did his duty.

Slocum saw that. He had sized up the lawman correctly, realizing that Shine was in trouble; maybe deep trouble. But that was not his affair, he was thinking to himself as he stood at the bar in the Elkhorn. A man had to look out for himself. Which was what he was doing. And why had Shine advised him that strongly to get out of town fast? Slocum wondered. Now, as he finished his whiskey, he had his moves set in his mind. With a nod at the bartender, he walked out. Five minutes later he walked into the Chip House.

The moment he spotted the room clerk he knew something was wrong. The man was in his thirties, with a short mustache, his brown hair parted in the middle, and he was wearing a starched collar with no necktie. The man said nothing, his face showed no expression, his voice was steady, he moved without hurry. Odd, even so. And then Slocum looked at his hands, detecting a tremor before the clerk dropped them beneath the desk.

"How many?" he asked.

The room clerk's pale face stiffened. "How many?" He cleared his throat, which was obviously dry; his words had come out almost soundlessly.

"How many visitors in my room?" Slocum said.

The man's surprise deepened into a flush. "I . . . I don't know. What do you mean, mister?"

Slocum suddenly reached across the desk and grabbed the clerk by his shirt. "Tell me! Right now! Who and how many upstairs. And where? In my room? In the hall? Where! Or I'll beat it out of you!"

The man was almost stammering as he said, "Four."

"Who? What names?"

"Dunno." He could barely get the word out, and had now started to shake.

Slocum let go of him. "You know. But you're more scared of them than you are of me, you damn fool. I'll let it pass this time. But next time, you tell me what I ask you. And if I find more than four up there, I wouldn't want anybody to be in your shoes."

He turned then, as though intending to start up the stairs. But almost immediately he turned back to the desk, catching the clerk in the act of throwing a quick, alarmed glance toward the top of the stairs.

"You're going up there," Slocum said, "and you will tell one of them—I am saying *one*—to come down here and I'll talk to him. Here." He pointed toward the corner of the lobby. "You got it? He'll go over to that chair and sit down. I will talk to him there. Now get upstairs!"

The clerk's face had turned from red to white and now gray. It was the color he wanted, Slocum decided. Gray meant he was too frightened to know anything more than the nearness of his own death.

Shaking, the clerk walked toward the stairs and,

holding the bannister began climbing to the floor above. Slocum watched for a moment and then walked quickly out of the hotel and onto the porch.

A glance told him no one was around. Even though it was dark, there was light thrown from the hotel and also from the building across the street. He had a good view.

He walked quickly to the end of the porch. Jumping up, he got a good hold on the drainpipe at the corner of the building and shimmied up to the roof of the porch. He figured the clerk would have reached his room by now, or at any rate someone waiting in the corridor outside his door. Bent over, and close to the side of the building, he moved carefully toward his window. The alley below had seemed deserted, and there were no lights in the windows he had to pass on the way to his own. In a minute he had reached the window of his room. It was dark, but suddenly there was light, and moving up close now but looking through the window at an angle so that no one inside could see him, he saw three men and the clerk standing in the open doorway.

But where was the fourth man? They certainly wouldn't have sent him downstairs alone. He had to be out in the corridor, didn't he? Slocum didn't hang on to that question, but with one punch of his gun barrel he broke the window glass and snapped, "Drop it!" to the man to his right who had spun, starting to draw as he did so.

There was a second of hesitation, and then the gun dropped back into its holster. Quickly, Slocum reached in, opened the window latch, and raised the window. Without taking a split second of attention away from his prisoners, he stepped into the room. "What's your name?" he said to the clerk.

"Edward."

"Go get that other one and bring him here."

"Yessir."

"If you're not back here by the time I count a minute, these three are going to be awfully sorry . . . plus you, my friend."

"Yes . . . yessir." And he was gone.

"That was dumb, inviting Turk for a powwow, Slocum. You figured we'd fall for that?" said the tallest of his three prisoners.

"It took your attention, mister. And I got back into my room. Now if he doesn't get himself right here real peaceful and fast like, then you three won't have to worry about it."

They were the kind he well knew—tough, mean, merciless, dumb yet wily.

"Right now, you unbuckle and drop those guns. Kick them over to me. Gently."

He watched them. He had moved well away from the window now. The tall man who had first spoken was looking at him through slitted eyes as he dropped his gun and belt to the floor.

"Pull your pants down. Fast!"

"What the hell!"

"Do it. Fast. All three." He raised the Colt slightly to underline his command.

They did it.

"Now you." He pointed to the one nearest the door. "Keep your pants down and walk to the door and tell your friend to come in."

"Slocum . . ."

"Right now."

The man he'd spoken to almost fell, moving to the door, as though he was wearing hobbles, which in a sense he was.

In a moment he was out in the corridor, but still within Slocum's view.

"That's far enough. Tell him to drop his gun and come on in. You hear me?"

"I hear you."

In the next moment Slocum heard him talking to the man out in the corridor.

"Tell him to come in slowly. Real slow. And Edward, too."

Slocum had his eyes on the remaining two men. Both were large and not the type who would be easy in a fight.

"Come in real slow," he called out now. "Edward, you go get Marshal Shine. Hurry it!"

The fourth man was even bigger than the others, though carrying a paunch that showed he wasn't in the best condition. But Slocum didn't let that lower his guard. He knew very well that some of those big paunchy men could be tough as boot leather.

"You think you outsmarted us, eh, Slocum," the new arrival said, his small mouth twisted in a sneer. He had close-cropped hair and a scar running down his left cheek.

"You drop your gunbelt and your pants. And we'll wait for the law."

"Bullshit. You ain't gonna get Shine to do a thing to us, don't you know that?"

"Turk, shut up," the man nearest him snapped. "Keep your big mouth shut, for Christ sake."

"I think he'll see it my way," Slocum said as he watched Turk drop his pants and like the others stand awkwardly in his longhandles. "I think we'll have a little conversation. What did you fellers want with me?" And he looked at them innocent as a newborn calf.

"We wanted to talk to you, Slocum," said the man who had told Turk to shut up.

"Four of you?"

One of the two who had not yet spoken made a sudden move, and in a flash Slocum had him covered. "I'll tell you when to move, mister. What's your name?"

"Hank."

"You?" He looked at the man standing beside him.

"Jerry."

"Goose," said the man who had spoken to the one named Turk.

"What do you want with us, Slocum?" Turk said, moving his hand slowly to scratch his belly button.

"I want you to tell me who sent you."

And then he heard the steps on the stairs.

But it wasn't Marshal Bill Shine who walked through the open door, nor was it Edward the room clerk. It was a short, round man, with a bald head and very bright blue eyes that reminded Slocum of a baby. And when those baby blues spotted the four standing there with their pants down, and in their longhandles, with those embarrassed looks on their faces, a great guffaw of laughter broke from that round body. He roared and he shook, quivering with uncontrollable mirth. Finally, and it seemed to Slocum with a magnificent display of willpower, he recovered. But it took a moment. He wiped his eyes, he shook his head as though unable to believe what he was seeing, and finally he beamed at Slocum.

"Mr. Slocum, I am ashamed to admit it, but these four individuals are, well, at least sort of in my employ. I do hate to say it, but they are. May we send them away? I am delighted to find this opportunity to discuss something with you of very great importance. And I, uh, would like so much to do that—to exchange with you on this vital matter, uh, before the Vigilance Committee of Fort Worth arrives."

The accent was very British, yet at the same time Slocum detected another inflection in the man's speech. German? French? He wasn't sure. And the emphasis on the words "Vigilance Committee" was not lost on him.

"I'd like first to be sure that you're not armed, and you can also tell me your name," Slocum said.

"Ah, forgive me. My name is Rumpel. Ralph Rumpel. How rude of me. Of course, I know your name. It's all over town, Mr. Slocum. And as I have just indicated, it has drawn the attention of the vigilantes. I'm sure you understand why we must talk rather to the point, and seriously. I should also like to point out that I am in a position to help you. And I, uh, am not armed." Sighing, he turned to watch the men who were still pulling up their trousers.

"Help me?" Slocum said, as he stepped forward and felt Rumpel for a hideout.

"Yes. You see, the Fort Worth vigilantes are very strong in town and in the surrounding country, too. They are also very strict—sometimes excessively so.

Some of them even appear to take pleasure in— what's that quaint Texas saying?—in, oh yes, in fitting malefactors with what they call a 'vigilante collar.'"

He beamed at Slocum as the door closed behind the departing men. "May I sit down, Mr. Slocum?"

2

"Interesting, is it not, Slocum, how one can so seldom rely on underlings to do anything correctly. Don't you find it so?"

"Rumpel, get to the point."

The round man grinned, not at all disturbed by Slocum's gruff manner. "Of course, Mr. Slocum. Of course. I realize I do tend to wander. But then, don't you know, life has so many interesting moments that for the creative individual it is often difficult to stay with the mundane facts of everyday existence. However..." And he chuckled, his blue eyes dancing in the light of the coal-oil lamp on the bedside table. "I will get to the point, of course. Of course!"

He was sitting on the edge of the bed, the only seat possible for him since Slocum had the chair, and was seated in it with its back toward his visitor.

"May I just say, Slocum, that's an interesting way in which you seat yourself. Ready to use the chair as a weapon, eh? Am I right?"

"Tell me what you want, Rumpel."

"I want to help you. I am sure you realize that you are, uh, unfortunately, and through no intention of your own, in trouble. It is big trouble."

14

"The vigilantes."

"The vigilantes. They have taken over the town. Marshal Bill Shine is powerless. Oh, they allow him to attend to minor law enforcement. Drunks, fist-fights, and all that sort of thing. But the real crimes, the banditti, the rustlers and road agents and mur-derers are handled exclusively by the Vigilance Committee."

"Who are they?"

Ralph Rumpel had thick, heavy, jet-black eye-brows, which looked as though they were holding up his forehead. These he now lifted in an attitude of questioning while he stuck out his lower lip. "No one knows the answer to that question, Slocum."

"That is bullshit, Rumpel. You know very well who's running the vigilantes."

The bed squeaked as the obese little man shifted his weight. He tried to make himself comfortable by crossing his legs, but his thighs were too big, and he gave up, slightly out of breath.

Slocum got a good picture of how the man could be impatient and damned hard to handle.

"Let me say this, Slocum." Rumpel pursed his thick, smooth lips. "Let me say that I enjoy a certain access to the vigilante situation. Nothing personal, you understand. Nothing personal. But I have been approached, no doubt because, with my connections in town here, I have often been considered a recon-ciling influence. You follow me?"

"I'd sure consider myself pretty damn dumb if I couldn't," Slocum said. "What you're saying is you've got a deal and I'm it. Otherwise . . ." He spread his hand, shrugging. "What is it you want?"

Ralph Rumpel had very prominent eyeteeth, and as he grinned now they came out of his mouth like fangs, giving him such a ludicrous appearance that Slocum wanted to laugh.

"I want you to drive three thousand head of Texas longhorns up to Montana. To Cold Rock. You know it? Near Antelope. I have heard of you, Slocum, and I know you're the man for the job. And not so by the way," he added, "the Vigilance Committee knows it too."

"And what's in it for me?"

Those black eyebrows lifted in surprise. "What's in it for you? Why, my good man, that is outstandingly obvious."

"I see."

"Uh, it might help if I touch your memory about a certain incident in—or at any rate near—Santa Fe. Uh, nothing proven, let us say, but something that could possibly cause embarrassment. At any rate, as you very likely know, there's a dodger on it."

"You're referring to the action with the Goldin gang, I take it, and my siding with the homesteaders."

"That is one way of putting it. But the stockgrowers still don't see it quite that way."

Slocum's grin was wicked. "The stockgrowers see things just like you, Rumpel. They see which side the money's stamped on."

Slocum leaned back in his chair, listening, his eyes on Rumpel. "I can hear that movement out in the corridor. I have to say you plan things pretty thoroughly, Rumpel."

"What do you say, Slocum?"

Smooth as water, John Slocum got to his feet. He stood looking down at the man seated on the edge of his bed. "How'd you know I was thinking of heading up north, Rumpel?"

The fat man grinned. "Just knew you'd see things my way sooner or later," he said as he started to get to his feet.

In the next instant Slocum had grabbed him by his collar and slammed him back onto the bed and straddled him, kneeling on his shoulders as he looked down into the man's suddenly glaring white face. "I said I was going to head north *anyway*. I'm not going because of you and your stinking vigilantes who don't have the guts to speak for themselves. But I will take your herd north—and you and those sonsofbitches will get the hell off my trail. You understand me?"

"Shit!" Rumpel gasped the word. He was sweating.

"I said, do you understand me?"

"I do."

Slocum released him. "It's understood I have a free hand," he said after Rumpel had seated himself again on the edge of the bed.

"Yes, agreed. But I have to know what you're doing. Listen, Slocum, I admire all your blood and thunder, and that is precisely why I decided to use you. But I want you to know one thing. I am not working with Boyd Flanagan." The words came out in gasps, for he was still short of breath.

"Boyd Flanagan?"

"You know him?"

"So it's Flanagan running the vigilantes."

"I am not with the vigilantes, though I sometimes find them useful." Rumpel was on his feet now, his chest still heaving. "And if it wasn't that I have a need for you, and your muscular approach to people, I assure you I'd have some of *my* men take care of you."

Slocum grinned at that. "Like those four, huh?"

Rumpel shook his round head. "Those fools. They just happened to be handy at a moment when I was pressed for time." He grinned suddenly, those fangs appearing like little tusks. "Slocum, I am working with a man in Montana named Hector Kinsolving."

"Never heard of him."

"He is the man who has ordered the beef. You will be delivering the herd to him. And it goes without saying that I will furnish you with enough good men for the drive."

"Those four included?"

Rumpel didn't answer. He was busy scratching the back of each arm in turn, losing some of his breath with the effort.

"I shall overlook your pugilistic behavior, Slocum, in the interest of forging ahead with my cattle plan. But I warn you, even though you may be considered extremely quick and accurate with a firearm, I shall have a *number* of men who are extremely quick and accurate." And with his face suddenly hard, no longer pudgy like a fat boy's, he straightened his clothing, shrugged his shoulders into his coat where it had become uneven, and then walked to the door and opened it.

Slocum's hand was close to his six-gun as he watched his visitor step across the threshold.

"One of my men will speak to you in the morning," Rumpel said, as he turned back to face Slocum.

"Boyd Flanagan?"

"For your information, once again I am *not working* with Flanagan. Or the vigilantes."

"Or are they working for you?" Slocum asked, though he didn't expect an answer. "Just remember, I find a one of them buggers or anybody else dogging my backtrail, he is going to be an awful sorry sonofabitch."

Ralph Rumpel took a moment to let that sink in, and then he said, "I just hope you're all you're said to be, Slocum—I mean, in all the saloons and gambling spots and the rest of Hell's Half Acre." The sneer was heavy in his words as he tried to regain a little of the lot he had lost.

Slocum's voice was as soft as a bird's as he said, "Gee, I sure hope so too, Rumpel."

In Fort Worth, Slocum had discovered that all Texas had the idea of driving cattle north. The reasons were clear. After the war Texans were broke, they needed federal money, and only cattle could get it for them. Slocum realized that dozens of herds were being made up. He saw too that the Texans had long been isolated from the rest of the country until the War Between the States, in which so many of them had fought, and now many were still bitter.

But Texas had the cowboys who could handle the longhorns, and Slocum quickly saw that Rumpel had gotten him a good crew, which did include the four who had broken into his hotel room. Still somewhat chastened, yet also somewhat unbowed, they were hands, after all, and they could be used. Slocum started the herd north, at first heading northeast on the Sedalia Trail that led toward Missouri and the Mississippi River, in order to avoid Indian trouble. At that time the Sedalia to Iowa and Illinois was the only decent trail known, a few herds having been driven over it before the war. But whatever the trail, as John Slocum already well knew, there was no more wild and unpredictable animal than the Texas longhorn. His herd proved the point again and again. The cattle would stampede at the least excuse, sometimes more than just once a night, and days were spent in rounding them up. Besides this problem, it was apparent that the Southwest had seldom known so wet a season. It rained constantly, and every thunderstorm caused a stampede. The ground had become so soggy that the men slept either in the saddle or in the mire. Every stream that they crossed was in flood, and the longhorns were famous for their dislike of water.

But Slocum had a good bunch of men. They were Texas cowboys all the way to the roots of their hair. At a riverbank a cowboy would kick his horse ahead as come-on bait and the other men would snap their leather-ended lariat ropes like whips at the cattle, urging them to follow. If the first got into the stream, there was a chance the others might follow. On the other hand, if they balked, whole days could be spent getting the beasts across.

It seemed the rivers and the stampedes were endless in the long, harsh miles they had to travel; and more often than not the men went without sleep, making good use of tobacco juice rubbed into their eyes to keep awake.

In the stampedes and in the charging currents of high water cowboys could easily get lost, injured, killed. This fact was known by all the men before they left Fort Worth, and Slocum knew it better than most. But thus far they had been lucky. Thus far not a man had been lost.

They were cutting back now, heading north and west, thus having avoided much, though not all, of the Indian land that was considered hostile, and so well worth avoiding even though it cost valuable time to do so.

Then one morning, about halfway toward noon, the herd stopped, and it seemed to Slocum, who was checking the drag, that they had stopped for good. Riding up ahead he soon found the trouble.

A great horde of longhorns was massed ahead, blocking the trail. On both sides the grass was eaten down to the roots and it was obvious that the cattle were soon going to be in trouble. Working his way around the mass of beeves, Slocum was confronted by a line of heavily armed horsemen, completely blocking the trail.

He swiftly sized up the brigands, obviously remnants of the Kansas Jayhawkers, sworn enemies of the Missouri bushwhackers in the guerrilla area of the recent war, who saw the cattle herds as money in their pockets.

"It's two dollars a head toll," the leader said. "And mind, there's a whole army of we-uns back apiece."

Slocum didn't argue. "We're heading for Booker

Wells," he told the bandit chief, a tall, lean man with a jet-black goatee, a gold ring in his left ear, four six-guns in his belt, and a Winchester rifle across the pommel of his saddle, plus a bowie knife in his boot.

"It's still two dollars a head."

Slocum rode back to camp and found a few of the men waiting for news.

"What happened?" someone asked.

Slocum told them.

"Ain't that a helluva note," an older hand said, and spat thoughtfully at a clump of sage.

"What we going to do, Slocum?" asked Turk, one of the four whom Slocum had confronted in his hotel room.

"We could beat our way through here," Slocum said. "Except if we take our men away from the herd, the cattle will be all over to hell and gone."

The older man who had already spoken moved in closer to Slocum. He sniffed. He had a curved nose, almost like a sickle. "We can whup the buggers, Slocum. I ain't one to allow such trash to backwater me, and I can see yourself ain't neither."

Slocum nodded in appreciation. "Know how you feel. But we get cut up, who'll drive the herd? Besides, if we dally here long enough they'll come for the cattle anyway."

"You figure they'll attack?" a young cowboy asked.

"No, not directly, but it could happen if we hang around long enough. They're not dumb. They know if they get to shooting up the cattle drivers then nobody'll come this way, so it won't hurt 'em to let us turn off the trail. But, thing is, I don't want 'em getting riled up by thinking about it too much. So since we got to get this herd up to Montana we'd best get our ass into leather and move west."

"But that there will be taking us right into more Indian country," somebody pointed out.

"That's what I know. But we'll be going by Leavenworth and I've got an idea," Slocum shot back. "Now, let's get this bunch of beef moving."

Then and there, the herd was started directly westward toward Indian territory. But Slocum knew it was going to be a tough one, for what he'd done was to trade Jayhawkers for Sioux.

They were lucky, he told himself, yet he knew it was also more than luck. The men had worked around the clock. There wasn't a man in the whole outfit who'd had a full night's sleep by the time they reached Fort Leavenworth. Here Slocum rested the cattle and his men. He bought wagons, ox teams, and groceries. Rumpel had given him plenty of money, which had made him suspicious of the man, but he didn't hesitate to spend it. He also hired some tough, dependable bullwhackers to skin his teams. And he met the C.O.

"I think you're crazy, Mr. Slocum, if you think you can get through the Sioux. They've got everybody pinned down up north. It's worse than here." It was Colonel Drine speaking, the commanding officer of Fort Leavenworth.

"I realize that, Colonel, but I'm going to give it a try."

"But man, you don't realize how strung up the Indians are. Washington only just made a treaty with

Falling Lance, and now the Army almost immediately has begun building a string of forts across Wyoming and into Montana. The Sioux naturally see this as a violation of their agreement, and they've hit the warpath." The colonel, a grizzled, gray-headed man, snorted.

"But it's the only way I can make it up to Cold Rock," Slocum pointed out.

"You've got as much chance as a virgin in a San Francisco cathouse," the colonel said. "But I see your mind's made up, and you don't look the type to get talked out of anything—or into it, either." And he smiled warmly. "I offer you hospitality, sir, but not much else."

"There is something I do need, Colonel Drine," Slocum said.

"Girls? They've got some cute ones—I have been told!—on the outskirts of town." He coughed into his fist. "They're highly competent, I have been told," he added, with extra emphasis on the last word.

"Thank you, Colonel, but I'm talking about some of those new Remingtons."

The colonel's thick gray eyebrows lifted in surprise. "Hah! One of the Army's best-kept secrets, I see." And he coughed, out a military laugh. "The breech-loading single-shots."

"The rolling blocks," Slocum said.

"You realize they are unknown out here in the West," Drine said.

"Almost unknown," Slocum countered.

The colonel's expression was wry. "It will have to

be absolutely unknown to anybody but the two of us."

"And my men."

"Of course. But understand, it's not against regulations, as long as we have a sufficient supply. It's just that I'm not anxious for the news to get around. Surprise is the element of survival—and not seldom," he added. "If I might take advantage of a western expression."

"Good enough," said Slocum with a grin, warming to the man.

"How many will you be wanting?"

"I have thirty men and myself. And of course we'll need a good supply of brass cartridges."

"I'll not be so worried about you then, Slocum," the colonel said, grinning. "Meanwhile, let's have a drink. I have some excellent whiskey right here in my desk."

Thank God for Philo Remington, Slocum was thinking as they pushed the herd north. At Fort Laramie he was again told by Army officers that his chances of getting through were slight indeed.

"Colonel Gallup is in charge up north of here," the C.O. at Laramie said. "He's building a new fort beyond Fort Reno, and he's got other sites selected. But where he is now the Sioux are killing his men and running off his horses daily. Gallup reports more than a thousand Indians around him. You've no chance at all on the Bozeman Trail, Slocum. The Sioux are determined to block it."

Slocum listened to the stories and kept his mouth shut. He knew he could still cut southwest to the

Oregon Trail, cross the divide into Idaho, and turn north, recrossing the divide, to Cold Rock. But that meant two high mountain passes, and the season was late. He could easily lose all his cattle in deep snow, and lose them without a fight. The trail that had been pioneered by John Bozeman was lower and two to three hundred miles shorter.

"I'm going on," he told the C.O.

"You're crazy, but I'm not going to stop you."

"That's what I know," Slocum said pleasantly. And they parted with a firm handshake.

At sunrise they were on their way, the three thousand longhorns and his thirty men with their thirty Remington rolling-block rifles. They soon learned what to expect. Several times they found charred remains of freight or emigrant parties, and mutilated bodies.

"You can see them watching us on the ridges," Slocum told one of the older cowhands, the man with a nose like a sickle. His name was Powder River Harold; a top hand in any man's book, Slocum allowed.

Then one quiet dawn, just after skirting Fort Reno, a large band of Sioux swept over a ridge and down upon the herd and riders. They came in close at full gallop, their horses' hooves drumming on the hard ground like thunder, and released a storm of arrows. Then they faded and reformed for a second charge. Two of the Texans—Goose Goslin and Slim Patches—had been hit and fell from their saddles.

Now the cowboys opened up with their Remingtons, and even they were surprised by the rapidity with which they could fire. Though greatly outnumbered, they poured it on. At last the wall of hostiles broke and gave way. The Remingtons had stood the test and had earned their victory for the drovers.

"We'll send word back to Reno for an ambulance," Slocum said as soon as he'd seen the extent of the wounds the two cowboys had suffered. When the ambulance arrived, the herd plus all the Texans moved to the fort.

It was clear to Slocum that the line of forts he'd been hearing about was indeed a reality. The army was building a line of containment, which he had to assume would then become a ring that would enclose the tribes and eventually wear them down to total surrender. It was not something he was pleased to contemplate—the extinction by slow attrition, with all the lies and deceit of the greedy invaders, of those so-called savages whom he respected, even though he'd had to kill his share. As just recently.

And indeed it was thanks to the Remingtons that he had succeeded. Otherwise, he wouldn't have had a chance against that superb cavalry, that unbelievable endurance and tenacity exhibited so impressively by the warriors of the plains.

The weapon was brand-new, with a breech that was opened by its rotating-block system, and which brought the block down and back and made reloading fast and easy.

Well, they were going to need not only the Remingtons from here on to Cold Rock, but a damn good piece of luck. And once again he was feeling that tingling in himself, along with the suppleness and ease of thought and physical movement that always came when he was in a tight spot. For instead of tightening up and so hampering his movement of body and thought, he always discovered that the more dangerous the situation he happened to be in, the more loose he was, the more able to maneuver. In short, he felt free. And it was a freedom he truly wished for.

At the same time he didn't let himself go soft with such thoughts. The frontier was no place for rumination or hesitancy. Slocum felt he understood some of the red man's ways because not only did he live in a similar manner but he had some Cherokee blood in his veins.

He knew he was going to need all of whatever he was if they were going to get the herd through. And as they moved farther north he found no lessening of his puzzlement over Ralph Rumpel and what the man might be up to. Was it simply cattle, opening a new route, more markets for beef? That in itself was a big order. But somehow Rumpel seemed a man who was going for even higher stakes than control of the beef shipments to the eastern markets. Big though that would surely become, Rumpel was no cattleman, and Slocum knew he had to have other irons in the fire.

No, it seemed the man must have a wider plan, and that the cattle drive was an aspect, an opening wedge. And who was Hector Kinsolving? Rumpel had said he was working with the man. The name had a strangely familiar ring in Slocum's memory, but he couldn't place it, no matter how hard he tried.

Then there was the question of his own place in the scheme. Why had Rumpel picked him? There were others who could drive cattle north, even longhorns. Rumpel had mentioned Santa Fe. Maybe the man had contacts there, for he'd used Santa Fe as a threat. It had been a tough one, going up against both John Goldin and the Schwemmer brothers. It was undoubtedly the Schwemmers who had gotten out the dodger on him.

Yet he could have gotten out of it. He could have gotten away from Rumpel and the Vigilance Committee, which was more than likely a cover for a lot of Rumpel's activity. He could have skipped Fort Worth. Except, on second thought, maybe not so easily, since Rumpel obviously did have some pretty fancy connections. No, his decision had been the right one. The trouble had been that he didn't know enough about the game that was being played, and so under the circumstances it had been the wise choice to play along with Rumpel and get away. Once up north, where he'd been thinking of going anyway, he would see what his next move should be.

At Fort Reno the men rested; the two wounded cowboys, after medical care, were soon able to ride. Since the feed was thin at Reno, Slocum saw that it was necessary to press on. He was looking forward to seeing what lay in store at Fort Tyson, and beyond that, his final destination—Cold Rock.

Once again the Army officers warned him that he'd never make it through the mass of Sioux that were determined to block the ring of forts that the Army was building. Scouts had reported that more and more Indians were joining Falling Lance.

The C.O., Colonel Mitchell, was not as insistent as the commanding officers at Leavenworth and Laramie had been. Slocum listened to the man and nodded agreeably to his warnings.

"I'm not insisting, Slocum," Mitchell said, "for I see clearly that you're one of those who makes up his own mind and sticks to it come hell or high water. So God be with you."

Slocum was relieved not to have to listen yet again to the warnings and veiled threats that he had endured from the Army at Laramie, and especially from the C.O. and his field officers. He knew it was useless to try to explain to the Army that their bulk and their very structure militated against the fluidity and speed of movement that a man in Slocum's position had at his disposal. Maybe Mitchell understood that. In any case, he got through without any orders being put out against him. Now, with the herd rested and his two cowboys on the mend, he pulled out. Even so, the warnings of the Army officers rang after him.

Fort Tyson was sixty-nine miles north. And though Indians were frequently seen along the way, they did not attack. Slocum wondered if word of the Remingtons had gone ahead. He had been told that the fort was still not more than three-quarters completed, but that work was going ahead at full steam in an effort to be buttoned down for the winter that would be coming.

All along the way Slocum knew that the Sioux were watching, and it was obvious too that their vigilance increased the closer the herd got to Fort Tyson.

Then about three miles from the near-completed fort soldiers stopped them.

"I have orders for you and your herd of cattle not to come any closer to the fort," the lieutenant in charge of the detail told Slocum.

"I want to know why, Lieutenant," Slocum said.

"Colonel Gallup's orders, sir."

"That does not answer my question," Slocum said firmly. "I said I want to know why."

The lieutenant was a young man, fresh from back east, quite obviously, for he flushed all over his face under Slocum's piercing look and hard words. "I believe it could be a matter of pasturage, Mr. Slocum. Colonel Gallup needs the feed for his own animals. But also there's a great danger—an increasing danger—building up farther north with the Sioux, and the Army doesn't have enough troops to protect civilians."

Slocum chose not to insist. "I'll be riding in to see the colonel," he said, "not that I have anything but respect for your orders, Lieutenant. But I will talk to Colonel Gallup personally about this matter."

And it had been left at that.

They camped, and that night at supper one of the men asked him why they didn't push through anyway, since that was more or less what they had done before.

"Two reasons," Slocum said, eyeing his questioner carefully. "Number one, we are facing a direct Army order. And number two, Gallup has three hundred men to enforce that order."

Without a sound the sun slipped toward the horizon of the tallest mountains, and now the light began to change more rapidly, touching the rifle barrel of the sentry on lookout at the gate of the unfinished fort.

And sunlight glistened too in the drops of water

beading the tawny grass of the rolling prairie. A jay called, and a flock of chickadees flew over the cattle herd just east of the fort. Now the last dying light washed the log walls that held Colonel Fabio Gallup and his three hundred officers and men, along with their weapons, their orders, their fear and courage, and their duty.

On the walls and at the lookout tower and gate, sentries watched for any sign of hostiles or other notable activity of the closing day. Nothing of note was expected, but it was always necessary to be alert to the unexpected, the difficult, and surely, as far as the Indians were concerned, the ambiguous.

The Indian ways were difficult for the white man to understand, though few whites if any mourned the fact. The natives were expected to bring to the authority of the fort, and the government it represented, nothing more than total submission. And it was seen by the whites as only a matter of time before this capitulation would take place. But meanwhile there were pockets of dissent among the original inhabitants of the raw and beautiful land, and there were as well the activities of the numerous banditti, resulting from the influx of former soldiers of the War Between the States, plus other opportunists seeking wealth and excitement where the law was thin, to say it modestly.

Indeed, the western hegira of the many good and useful citizens seemed heavily outnumbered by the gamblers, the bunco artists, the highwaymen and murderers, as well as those legal purveyors of "Manifest Destiny" who preyed upon everybody.

As for the law, there were the U.S. marshals, but

these were few, as were the sheriffs and other local constabulary. And of course among the upholders of the law there were those who were not wholly devoted to the honesty and courage that was expected of them. There were some truly fine lawmen, and there were the less fine, and there were the corrupt.

And there was the Army. But the Army was understaffed, and was principally there in order to maintain peace with the natives. And although these facts were well known in all corners of the West, Colonel Fabio Gallup was nevertheless going over it again as he and John Slocum faced each other across the commanding officer's desk.

Slocum had been more than glad for the opportunity to rest his longhorns, but at the same time he was not interested in delaying the final leg of his drive to Cold Rock. Things had gone reasonably smoothly as they'd moved through Leavenworth, Laramie, and the edges of the Sioux country. But it was beginning to look like Gallup might become a stumbling block. The man was long-winded, to say the least.

"Before we go any further, Mr. Slocum, I have got to reiterate my point that you are making a very big mistake in thinking that you can get through Falling Lance's Sioux."

"We have managed thus far, Colonel," Slocum said. "Even though outnumbered, our weaponry made up for the difference—I'd say in spades."

The colonel cleared his throat. He was a man who seemed to Slocum as built like an iron bar, obviously born in uniform, at military attention as he arrived in the world. Slocum did not feel negative about the fact. He knew very well how much the western conquest depended upon such Army men, though he did not necessarily agree with it. He also knew how such sticklers could tie up an action until dry rot set in.

"The Sioux," Gallup was saying as he ponderously dropped his words across his desk toward his visitor, "are more than just restless. They're damn well riled, and it is definitely not the time to try pushing three thousand head of cattle up through the territory. Most especially when you could be crossing land allotted to the hostiles. It is that possibility, sir, that militates—to my mind, mind you—against giving my permission." He paused, but it seemed only in order to gather momentum. "I, uh, say the word 'possibility,' for I am quite sure you wouldn't intentionally cross onto Sioux land."

Incredibly, the colonel paused, as though he intended to listen to what Slocum might have to say. Slocum had heard of Fabio Gallup. The man was known for his rigidity, his hewing to the book. He had fought on the Union side during the late war. A man in his early forties, a touch of gray at the temples, a full brown mustache, side choppers, but a clean chin.

Slocum had taken note of the framed drawing of a woman on the colonel's desk. Wife? Daughter? it added a dimension to the military man with the hard face, the iron shoulders.

Slocum leaned a little forward in his chair. "What are you telling me, Colonel?"

"I am saying I could order you not to head north. I could order you to turn your herd around, to take a longer trail."

"But you're not going to."

Slocum's fast comeback brought the streak of a wry grin to Gallup's face, which he dropped instantly. "Uh, let's not be so certain." His hand moved along the top of his crowded desk, fingers tapping lightly. Then they stopped, his arms stretched out as he leaned slightly on the heels of both hands and regarded his visitor carefully from beneath strict eyebrows.

"You have three thousand beeves for market, Mr. Slocum. And those beeves couldn't last very long on the feed that's around here. And if you should turn around and head back to Texas, you'd still have the Sioux. I'd wager an educated figure that they've got you cut off from the rear." He tapped a forefinger onto a random piece of paper. "You see, I am trying to be cooperative, Slocum."

"I fully appreciate that, Colonel."

"I somehow feel you should have a chance at driving them to a market. The longhorns shouldn't be allowed to die of starvation simply because of a lot of goddamn bloodthirsty savages. Ah, if only I had another company of the caliber we had when we broke Pickett's charge. It would be a different story, that I assure you." His dark eyes suddenly brightened; his Adam's apple pumped in his throat.

For a moment Slocum thought Gallup was going to say more about his war experience. The man had definitely touched something in himself at the reference to a wartime engagement. But the moment passed.

"You should have a chance. Your fate, Slocum, is momentarily in my hands, and I shall offer you quarter. Mind you, I don't believe you have a chance of a candle in hell, but you seem determined."

"That I am, Colonel. And so are my men."

Colonel Gallup cleared his throat, leaned slightly forward, and regarded Slocum with an expression that was now totally neutral. "You have told me that you have only men in your party. No women, no children. I presume that all your men have agreed to go along, that they are fully aware of the conditions lying ahead, the risk, the possibility—nay, the likelihood—that they will meet their Maker ere very long. But so . . . !"

He leaned back, again leveling his somber eyes at Slocum. "In other words, if everyone in your party understands the risk he will be taking, and still agrees to be a part of it, then I shall not stand in your way. I won't object. But I will say again that you are being very foolish. Damned foolish, sir! And—stubborn!"

"Well, I sure can't take 'em back to Texas," Slocum said.

"Let me put it this way," Gallup went on. "I will necessarily have to order you to turn around and go back, or, that is, order you not to push through to the Bozeman trail. And in fact, that is what I am doing. The rest is up to you. I can only wish you Godspeed."

"Got it," Slocum said.

"Let's be clear, then. Officially I have told you not to drive your herd through Sioux country."

"That is what I have heard, Colonel."

"Then we understand each other. Good enough."

But Slocum could see that there was something

more that the colonel had not yet divulged. He waited.

Suddenly Gallup bent down to his left and opened a small cupboard door in his desk. He came up with a bottle and two glasses. As he poured, he said, "We are able to offer only small pleasures here, I'm afraid. But . . ." He held up the bottle for Slocum to see. "It's a good one, I think you'll agree."

"I'll be glad to give it a try." Slocum grinned, pleased to see that Gallup had something of an other side to his character. The man had to be more than just a rule book.

And it was good. It went down smoothly.

"Not the average brand of trail whiskey," Slocum said, as his stomach warmed.

Fabio Gallup smacked his lips. "It's prime stuff. Expensive. Guess where it's from."

"Frisco? K.C.?"

The colonel put his glass firmly on the desk. "The Bozeman Trail. Or close by, at any rate. Crazy Woman Creek."

"Whiskey trader."

Gallup nodded, fingering his trim mustache, and then sniffed at the tips of his fingers. "It was quite a shipment."

"Well, it's a business," Slocum said laconically. "I'm not surprised."

"It's big. It's a big business, Slocum."

"I'm aware of that."

"Sure. I'm sure you are. But it's getting worse."

"They selling it to the Indians?"

"So far it's been mostly the regular markets. But this shipment was discovered on Sioux land. I have every reason to believe that somebody is getting whiskey to the tribes. Not necessarily selling it, you understand. Giving it. Getting them stirred up. You know how the Indians are with whiskey."

"I do," Slocum said. "They're too damn healthy to be able to tolerate it. They've never been used to it. It's simple."

"Of course."

"But why are you telling me all this?"

"I am doing you a favor. Remember?"

Slocum said nothing, but he was watching Gallup carefully. Then he said, "And what is the favor I am doing you, Colonel Gallup?"

"I want you to keep your eyes open. If you see anything suspicious I want you to let me know." He took a drink while Slocum remained silent. "Remember, I am doing you a favor."

"I see that you're not going to let me forget it, Colonel," Slocum said with a slow smile.

At that the colonel barked out a laugh and lifted his glass in a toast. Returning his glass to his desk, he cocked his head at Slocum and said, "I see that you have Remingtons. I'm not quite as worried about you as I had been. Nevertheless, be careful. Be really careful. And, uh, see what you can discover for me. Oh, and by the way, I almost forgot." He took another pull at his whiskey. "It damn near slipped my mind. There's a covered wagon pulled in down by the creek. In fact, three wagons. Some kind of a circus. I understand they're heading for Antelope." He stood up unexpectedly and walked over to a map on the wall behind Slocum, who turned in his chair. "Antelope is no more than a half day out of your way. In fact, I'd say it was almost along your route, yet not within Indian territory. I do believe the circus people are heading there. And it might be a place for you to stop over. Of course, that's up to you." He crossed back to his desk and sat down again. "Entirely up to you, Slocum. But please remember if you hear anything on that whiskey business, I will be grateful, not to mention the Army of the West's gratitude."

It was in that brisk and very sudden "afterthought" that Slocum saw his man. Fabio Gallup was no dummy, and certainly he was a lot more than the average military man. He would let him go through with his longhorns if he investigated the Conestogas and reported on his findings. Slocum got to his feet absolutely convinced that the colonel had a lot more up his sleeve than simply building Fort Tyson and holding the Sioux at bay. But he knew he and his cowboys also had a lot on their own plates during the next few days. Interesting, for sure, how the colonel had mentioned the fact that he had Remingtons. No question but that the man was shrewd. And as he walked away from Colonel Fabio Gallup's quarters, Slocum suddenly thought of Ralph Rumpel. He had the strangest feeling that somehow there had to be a connection between the two men. By the time he got back to the cattle and his cowboys he'd decided that it wouldn't be so much out of the way to swing by Antelope. By the time they got up in that area the men and cattle both would be needing some rest. Then from there up to Cold Rock would be a fairly short drive, and he didn't want the longhorns to reach their destination gaunted and with their ribs showing. And besides, he'd heard of Antelope; he remembered now that Rumpel had mentioned the place. He'd have to think about that, for he couldn't remember exactly what the man had said, only that it had been strangely casual.

3

No question but that she was about the best-looking thing Slocum had seen in a good while. Tall though not too tall, curving in just the right places, with just the right angles, she crossed from the covered wagon over to the cook fire with the grace of a deer, the excitement of everything a man could think of. Blond hair, high cheekbones, flashing amber eyes, and the tip of an earlobe just beneath some wisps of hair that told him her ears had to be perfect. For what could possibly be imperfect in such a creature?

He knew she knew he was staring at her, yet she didn't once look his way. He had spotted her as he led his pony down to the three Conestogas that were standing at a bend in the winding creek. The colonel had said they were a circus, but carnival would have been a closer description, Slocum realized as he watched the activity. For a moment he'd thought they might be gypsies, but he soon realized they were carny folk; and anyway, he'd never heard of a blond gypsy. He wondered what she did in the carnival. Looking at her he just wondered.

He continued to stand there by the team of oxen, who were immobile in their heavy harness, as a

41

young boy unhitched them from the Conestoga and led them away.

Now somebody rolled a barrel across the churned-up grass, stopping almost at the center of the camp ring made by the wagons. Everywhere was activity. Men were setting up tables; women were cooking over a fire that had recently been built. Slocum watched as the girl took up her station at the barrel that had been rolled out. He realized now that a number of soldiers were watching as he was, standing about in little knots, commenting on the activity that was taking place. Obviously the carnival, or whatever it was going to be—a theater, a lottery, gambling—was getting into action.

The blond girl had taken a deck of cards from somewhere in her skirt and had started to shuffle on the barrel head. Some of the soldiers approached as she looked up and smiled at them.

"Gentlemen! You boys feel in the mood for a little fun? Some good, clean sport?"

"Sure as hell do," said a voice near Slocum, and a three-striper walked past him, beaming with anticipation as he looked at the monte dealer.

"I'll take a crack at it, miss," Slocum said suddenly. He hadn't expected to speak, but the girl had suddenly looked at him, and he felt that familiar clutching in the pit of his stomach and loins.

The crowd had grown as more soldiers appeared and more of the wagon train entered into the activity. There was a small tent being raised at a side of the ring, and as Slocum looked over he saw a sign that stated that fortunes would be told for two bits.

But he had his attention fully on the three-card

monte game now as he pushed in close to the blond with the fast and, it appeared, highly adroit hands.

"Which one's the ace? Here you see it. Here you don't. Which one's the ace? Gents, try your luck. Put your money on the card."

Slocum won a couple, lost a couple. Then he lost, and lost again. He knew it was time to quit. But he was finally able to follow how she did it. The men around him were having similar luck. Yet he knew none of them could follow her hands. At any rate, no one said so. And it occurred to him then that maybe she was letting him see her cheating. Of course, since cheating was the name of the game, it couldn't be called "cheating." The hand *was* quicker than the eye. And if he hadn't had as much experience as he'd had over the years watching three-card monte dealers he would never have seen it now.

"Here's the ace. Now you see it." And her hands were a blur. Or were they? They didn't seem to move all that fast. Yet they did, and the attention of the players and onlookers was lost.

"Which one's the ace?"

Her smile brought them all to their knees. Gladly. She could have emptied their pockets, unbuttoned their flies, stripped them to their birthday suits, and no one would have raised a squeak of protest.

Only it wasn't all smiles and soft soap, nor horny customers. The girl was a true professional, he could see that clearly. And now again as he began to win more than a rare one, he was sure she was leading him on. For a killing? Slocum didn't care. And when he quit the game, with his winnings and the admiration and even awe of his fellow players, he knew he 'wasn't in all that much hurry to hit the trail to Antelope and Cold Rock.

Indeed, that was exactly what he told the young lady later.

"I don't reckon I'm in all that much hurry to hit the trail north," he said as she rolled over on top of him again and whispered her invitation into his ear.

"I really didn't think you were," she said, as she slipped her wet vagina down along his rigid shaft, then reached behind herself to grab it in her hand and stroke, keeping time with her pumping buttocks.

"I want to be on top this time," she whispered.

"That's what I figured," Slocum said. And he slid his erection all the way into her as she spread her legs even wider and wiggled and began to gasp as he drove in and up and around, and slid back, and then drove in and up again—smooth as a dance he brought her again to her gasping, pumping climax as he flooded her with come and she poured hers all over his belly.

They lay locked together, with soft hands and legs, resting, sighing with the exquisite relief at releasing all that had been building during the monte game.

"Have you got a name?" he said when she lifted her head and looked down into his face.

"I don't like names."

"I'm Likes-to-Come-Lots," Slocum said.

"You Injun too, huh?"

"Sometimes."

Her laughter tinkled down into his face as they began pumping together. After a moment he flipped her onto her back, but he didn't enter her right away. Instead he raised her leg so that he entered her from behind while lying on his side next to her.

"I like riding sidesaddle," she said, barely able to speak the words as the intensity of her delight took over completely. And now she was gasping with each thrust as he drove in, and she squirmed under the impact of his probing member.

Then she was turned away from him as he stroked in and got her up onto her hands and knees and from behind rode her beautifully to their second climax.

They slept a little then, and then they did it again. And finally Slocum got up, bending his head so that he wouldn't hit the canvas top of her Conestoga.

"It was real good," he said as he buttoned his pants.

"You didn't have to say that, Slocum."

"It was good," he said again.

She gave a little laugh, then reached over to check the coal-oil lamp which had started to smoke a little. "I like stubborn men."

"I like girls."

"Not choosy? I don't believe that."

"I never met a woman that I didn't get to know better by bedding her," he said.

"You are stubborn." And she gave another little laugh, but there was a bit of surprise mixed in it.

"Hunh," he said, buttoning his last button.

"You're saying all skunks are gray in the dark."

"That what you think of men?"

"What kind do you think I mostly meet dealing monte?" She sniffed and sat up on the bed, her breasts falling into the lamplight. "But I don't read you that way. You're different."

Suddenly he said, "How did you know my name was Slocum?"

"I don't know. Didn't you tell me?"

"No, I didn't."

"I . . . I dunno."

"You heading for Antelope?"

"I don't know. It depends on Dutch. He's the man with the fuzzy balls."

"Dutch?"

"Wagner. He runs the outfit."

"Has he got any more girls as pretty as you?" Slocum said, buckling his gunbelt.

"That's something you'd have to figure out, Mr., uh, Slocum did you say the name was?" And she was cocking her head at him, her tongue pushing out her cheek, and there was a sly look in her eyes which seemed also to be dancing with hardly suppressed laughter.

"I like the cut of your rig," he said then. "Maybe I'll run into you someplace."

"Maybe."

He stepped toward the opening at the end of the wagon. He could feel the predawn coming into the sky outside, and the land, without actually seeing it. It was that sense he had. He had had it ever since he could remember, the awareness of himself and his surroundings. It was the sense that could know the presence of danger, or its opposite. As now.

"My name's Norah," she said as he started to step outside.

"Pleased to meet you, Norah." He grinned at her,

sensing there was something more in her remark than just her telling him her name. And he still wondered how she had known his name.

As he stepped down from the wagon, the faintest light was touching the eastern sky, and the air was cool.

At a glance, Antelope's Lead Dollar Saloon certainly lived up to its name. The last sunlight was covering the town as Slocum walked into its gloomy interior. He had been in funeral parlors that were more lively. The trail whiskey that the tube-shaped barman poured him supported his view. It was a fight to get it down his throat, but he managed. After the long haul from Fort Worth and various points along the way, he figured he had earned something, even though poisonous.

It was so gloomy in the room that he could barely make out the people as he stood at the bar wondering whether or how soon he might see some of his Texas cowboys. He'd only just ridden into town, alone, after having given orders for the herd and the wagons. He knew some of the men were in town; he'd sent them. But they were obviously at some other—and he hoped more favorable—watering spa.

It was just at this point in his reflections that a door burst open at the far side of the room and the fiddled strains of lively dance music strutted in, loud and appealing, along with shouting, laughter, and the general clamorous noise of what could only be described as good times.

Slocum was about to pick up his drink and make

for the more alive part of the Lead Dollar when he realized that a man had come through the door and was approaching him. He was a fleshy man, though not fat, almost bald, and clean-shaven, with a red face that looked as though it had been burned.

"Matt Otto is the name. You're John Slocum. Al just told me you were here. Welcome to Antelope—the kindest town this side of the Rockies." He shoved his thick hand forward onto the bar in signal to the man on the sober side. "Al, Mr. Slocum here wants a drink of whiskey, not this grizzly piss you been serving." And he pushed Slocum's glass away. "Don't drink that rotgut, Slocum. While you're in Antelope, you'll be served the best."

"I appreciate it, Otto."

"Matt. Or you can call me Magic. Magic Matt Otto—hah!—at your service."

"And it's you who named Antelope the kindest town this side of the Rockies?"

"I did, sir. I did indeed. How'd you know it?"

"Guessed."

Magic Otto beamed.

"How did you really know my name, Magic?"

A rich chuckle bubbled up from the other man's chest. "To tell you the honest-to-God truth—and I got to say, telling the truth is a habit with me; been that way since I was a shaver—to tell you the truth, I got friends all over the West. Got the reputation for being friendly."

"And honest."

"Right. Right you are!" And Magic nodded vigorously, beaming at Slocum.

"One of those friends happen to be a United States

Army colonel?" Slocum asked innocently.

Magic Otto's beam broadened. He overflowed with warmth and goodwill—his own private sun. "The colonel is one of my closest—I say closest—friends, Slocum. And that is an honest-to-God fact."

"I do believe you," Slocum said.

"The colonel suggested I offer you hospitality, which I would more than likely be doing even if he hadn't said so, on account of I can see you are a man cut from the same cloth as myself." He turned, or rather he seemed to roll away from the bar, his open hand sweeping the dull room, but evidently including the noisy adjoining premises. "We ain't much out here in the end of nowheres, but we keep up to our slogan; and I must say, we have got something more than just nothin'. I'd bet my last roll on that."

"Obliged," Slocum said.

"Make yourself to home, then. Let me know anything you got to have." And a big chuckle came all the way up from deep in his chest and broke close to Slocum's quiet face. "There is poker, three-card monte, faro, dice—you name it and we got it. Not forgetting the girls. We have got the friendliest girls this side—no!—*either* side of the Rockies." And he broke into a roar of laughter, slapping his hand against the top of the bar and almost spilling his drink.

"Slocum, I say let me know what you need." And with another huge grin all over his shiny face he moved down to the other end of the almost silent room, nodding, saying a word here and there as he went.

Slocum took a pull at his drink. Gallup. Yes, there

was something extra about the man. He'd thought it at the time of their meeting, and he felt it again now. The question was, why was Magic Otto giving him the glad hand? Was he that way with every passerby? True, there were three thousand head of Texas cattle out there, and so he wasn't coming into Antelope empty handed, as it were. But what could Magic expect from him? Was he somehow connected with Rumpel?

There appeared no immediate answer to his questions, so he decided to let it all ride. He would simply keep alert to what was happening, and see what events could tell him. And so he decided to accept the saloonkeeper's hospitality and enjoy himself. First step, then, was to take a look into the neighboring room, where the big action seemed to be taking place.

And it was. The dance floor was jammed, and so were the gaming tables. In fact, the room was really the main part of the establishment, for there was a huge bar running along one side. There was an orchestra, and there were gaming tables of the usual and expected variety.

Now Otto appeared and opened the door wide to the second, quieter room which Slocum had just left, thus making passage easier for his customers, of which there seemed to be a considerable overflow. The place was jammed.

Watching Magic Otto now, Slocum remembered he had heard of him—a man with a genius for the dice, a golden arm, and he was reputed to be able to switch tops and flats right in the midst of the hottest action without the quickest eye spotting him. Yes, known as the fastest draw north of the Rio Grande.

Slocum made it through the crowd to the big bar at the far end of the room and ordered another drink. He was beginning to enjoy himself, though not losing his vigilance, for he felt there was more to Antelope and Gallup's suggestion that he stop by than he was seeing at the moment. And what about Rumpel? Was there a connection between Rumpel and Magic Otto? Why had Rumpel mentioned Antelope? Or was he just seeing a problem that wasn't really there?

Obviously, though, Rumpel had something bigger in mind than just his three thousand head of cattle getting to market. Only where did Slocum fit in? Why had Rumpel wanted him for his cattle drive? And for what else besides? It surely wasn't just accident that they had met.

"Lively, ain't it?" said the voice beside him.

"That it is." Slocum nodded at the profile of the angular man with the face that looked as though it was carved from stone. The sharp gray eyes only accented the granite quality of the whole face, which was slightly pinched, too, reminding Slocum of a wolf. Nor did he fail to notice the Smith & Wesson in the worn holster at the man's hip. It was one of those guns that looked as though it was part of the person wearing it.

The man had a grainy voice, his words seeming to come from the back of his throat. And those words were arid as a desert.

"Kind of place for people who don't want to be where other people do want 'em to be," he said, keeping his words close to his mouth. "Name's Roller."

Slocum said nothing and felt the man withdraw. He watched him moving along the bar from the corner of his eye, but now he turned his attention to the two wheels of fortune, the big dice game, the poker tables filled with players. The room was thick with smoke, noise, the body smell of men, and now and again a trace of feminine perfume and brassy laughter. The girls, he noted, were busy, and as he watched one of them escorting a male companion upstairs to one of the rooms off the balcony, he thought of Norah and wished that she was in town. Then he wondered if she would be.

But now his attention was taken by the faro dealer setting up his bank just a few feet away from where he was leaning against the bar. He noted that the man who had called himself Roller was also watching the dealer, who was a small man standing straight as a string beneath his shiny brown derby hat. He wore a richly brocaded vest over a striped shirt, the sleeves of which were gripped just above the elbows by a pair of bright red garters. A big gold watch chain swung across his flat stomach, and as he bent over his worktable it hung down.

Slocum enjoyed watching the professional touches of the faro dealer as he set up. It was one of the things he always liked about gambling halls—the manner in which a man worked his cards or dice, showing the same care a good cowhand showed in topping out a tough bronc or roping a calf out of a herd for branding. It was always satisfying to watch a man working when he really knew his business and respected it. He could see that a man like the little faro dealer not only knew the game he would be dealing backward, forward, and inside out, but he would know more than that. He would know the people he was playing with. It was this that especially interested Slocum. For him, the game was in playing the people, the other players. And it was beautiful to watch.

He continued to observe the dealer preparing his setup with his assistant, who would be the one to pay and collect the bets, and his casekeeper, who would manipulate the small box that contained a miniature layout with four beads running along a steel rod opposite each card. It would be the casekeeper's job to move the beads along, as on a billiard counter, as the cards were played, so that the players could immediately tell what cards remained to be dealt.

Slocum studied the extra care with which the dealer now placed his layout—the suit of thirteen cards, all spades, painted on a large square of oilcloth. The cards on the layout were arranged in two parallel rows, with the ace on the dealer's left and the odd card, which was the seven, on his far right. Enough space was allowed between the rows for the players to place their bets.

In the row closest to the players were the king, the queen, and the jack, called "the big figure" in faro talk, and the ten, the nine, and the eight. Then, in the row that was nearest the dealer, the ace, deuce, and trey, "the little figure," and the four, five, and six. Slocum remembered that the six, seven, and eight were called "the pot," the king, queen, ace, and deuce were called "the grand square," the jack, three, four, and ten were "the jack square," and finally the nine, the eight, the six, and the five were "the nine square."

Fully appreciating the way the dealer set his layout, Slocum watched as he shuffled, cut the deck, and placed the cards face upward in the dealing box, the top of which was, of course, open.

The dealer straightened his shoulders, his preparations concluded. "Faro!" he called out. "Faro bank open!"

And all at once Slocum felt the urge to play. He was, in fact, struggling with himself, for he also wanted to remain detached and be able to observe the scene, when again he heard a voice behind him. Except that this time it was a different voice.

"Is the gentleman enjoying it?"

Turning, he discovered the speaker was one of the women his eye had caught only fleetingly as he'd first walked into the room. And right now he was staring into a pair of catlike hazel eyes under a rush of carrot-colored hair that tumbled down onto bare marble shoulders and beyond, reaching to a pair of wholly formidable breasts that seemed to be the sole means of supporting the green satin dress. This sensuous garment, molding itself over the pair of prominent nipples, outlined in the most delicious detail such an animal body as he had ever encountered. That was all there was; nothing else was needed. The conversation that ensued seemed to Slocum quite superfluous, yet he stayed right with it. It sure beat drinking alone, he told himself as he tore his eyes away from those nipples to meet the divine creature's lynx-like appraisal.

"Is it all right?" she asked in a voice that held a trace of some foreign accent.

"So far."

An eyebrow was raised. "How far do you wish?"

"Depends."

"Depends on what?"

"I reckon," Slocum said, "on how far we just so far have been."

Without appearing to move, she was suddenly closer. "How far have we been, then?" she asked innocently.

"I'd say a good piece of the way, only not far enough."

"I don't know what you're waiting for, mister."

"I dunno either," Slocum said. "It sure ain't for Christmas, or permission from Mom."

Slocum was feeling the familiar heat in his loins as he put down his glass.

And it was just at this point that a woman screamed, "Get away from me, you pig!"

"Bitch! Whore! Cut it out!"

The man's voice touched Slocum's memory, and then to his astonishment he saw that it was the voice of Link Rudabaugh, he whom he had backwatered, beaten, and whipped to the floor back in Fort Worth. He was standing in front of a plump, dark-haired girl whose dress was ripped down the front so that her bare breasts were exposed to the entire room, and especially to the gleaming eyes of her tormentor.

Slocum took a hard second look at the man. Obviously he'd ridden up ahead of the cattle drive. Was there any connection? Were others with him? Maybe the man had simply followed the drive. But that wasn't likely, for he had ridden the drag himself and checked their backtrail diligently. No, he would have spotted any sign. And maybe Rudabaugh had come by stage. That was still a rough travel, but better than horseback and in the cattle drag. And maybe his being at Antelope was coincidence. But seeing Rudabaugh reminded him again of Ralph Rumpel and the question of what the man was up to. Rumpel had made a point of telling him he had gunmen at his command. Was Rudabaugh one of them? Was he up here scouting the cattle drive to see if Rumpel's orders were being followed?

Slocum's thoughts were roughly interrupted as a shout went up and a large man pushed his way through the crowd, roaring at Rudabaugh.

"You keep yer mitts offa my property, you Texas sonofabitch!" And with knotted fists he bore down on the defiler of sexual property.

Clearly the man was long on muscle and a tough customer all around, but it was also very clear that he was short on intelligence. The room, now with a half dozen of Slocum's own men there from the cattle drive, bore witness to this fact. No man of any sense whatever would use such language as "Texas sonofabitch" in front of even a small number of those individuals who referred to their homeland as "Takes-Us." Not anyone who expected to be around later to tell about it.

The speaker of the blasphemy was now right in front of Rudabaugh and all at once unleashed a kick aimed at the Texan's crotch. But Link, even though mightily liquored, was still enough with himself to avoid the big boot, and he now countered with a smashing overhand right to the big man's jaw. His adversary didn't blink. Rudabaugh could as well have hit a stone wall.

In the next instant the Texas yell hit the room, shaking the walls, the ceiling, and the floor, and the big fight was on. Someone grabbed a bungstarter and smashed the huge defender of his lady friend's virtue in the back of his neck, dropping him to his knees. A chair swept through the room and drove Rudabaugh into the orchestra, at which point the musicians— momentarily frozen into immobility—regained their reflexes and stepped into a racing rendition of "The Star Spangled Banner." Both rooms were now a battling mass of humanity.

Slocum remained absolutely quiet beside the girl, who was also motionless, though he could feel her fear. They were standing just at the edge of the fray.

"Upstairs, the balcony. Second on the right," she said, keeping her eyes straight ahead. And she was gone.

Slocum ducked a bottle that came hurtling in his direction, only to be clipped from behind as a man hit the backs of his knees, and he was down. His attacker was a tough one, but an aggressive elbow in his crotch, followed by a chop in his Adam's apple, disposed of him, and Slocum was up on his feet.

The fiddlers and piano player were still punishing the anthem at top speed, and Slocum saw the man who had called himself Roller, he with the face like a block of carved granite, standing rigid as a soldier at attention, right in the center of the melee, his right hand and arm frozen in salute, while the battle raged all around him and the musicians reached a frenzy in their effort to stop the tide. But Roller stood there in honor of either his country or possibly his lost cause. Yet for but a brief moment of glory. One of Slocum's drunken young cowhands smashed him over the head with a full bottle, and, still saluting, he sank in blood and Old Overholt to the floor. His assailant was instantly swept from the action by a flying chair.

Slocum had now reached the stairs leading to the balcony, where he found his way blocked by two burly bruisers. One of them looked vaguely familiar, but he didn't take time to search his memory, for the man swung a short, powerhouse right at his jaw. His companion tried to grab Slocum around the waist so that he could backheel him. Both efforts reaped failure as Slocum, agile as a mountain cat, dropped both adversaries to the floor, out cold.

Slocum felt pretty good then as he settled into the fight. But he didn't stay with his pleasure; there was the girl waiting for him. The battle would simply wear itself out in due course. Throwing a chair at the legs of a man who charged him, he leaped to the stairs and raced up to the balcony. After all, it was time for the right priorities. Definitely.

And suddenly the thought flashed through his mind: Where was Magic Otto during the festivities?

She was already in bed when he got to her room. The covers were pulled up to her chin; yet covered, Slocum felt her as appealing as any of the most passionate women he had known.

"Lock the door, will you," she said.

Half turning, he turned the key in the lock, his eyes on her, as she sat up in the bed holding the sheet to cover her breasts. Suddenly he felt the old familiar rush going through him. And in the next moment he knew what it was.

"Toss the key on the bureau, will you, hon."

But he didn't. He left it crossways in the lock so it couldn't be pushed out, his eyes still on her, seeing the light flush come to her cheeks. He stepped quickly to the window and looked out into the alley and street. It was a corner room, and there was a rain barrel just below.

She was sitting up in bed now, her high, firm breasts bare to his view. "Nobody can get in here, if that's what you're worried about," she said.

"But I can get out," Slocum said as he threw his leg over the windowsill. "So long. Sorry to miss the hayride," he said as he heard the sound of movement outside the door of the room.

"What the hell are you doing!" she cried out, throwing off the sheet and jumping up out of bed to stand naked before him.

"I'm saying so long, miss. Nice try, but it was as obvious as those cute tits you're pushing at me. Tell the boys they've got to do better than that."

Swiftly, he swung over to grab the rain pipe and then slid down to the rain barrel directly below. As he ran along the alley he heard the man's shout from the bedroom window.

"Stop, thief!"

Slocum didn't look back. He was just glad there were no gunshots. At the same time he was sorry to miss those wonderful breasts and all the rest of it.

4

And so they were still at it. Target: John Slocum. Obviously the girl had been in on it. Had Otto? Was it connected with Link Rudabaugh? And was Rudabaugh working with Rumpel? If that was the case, why would Rumpel want him bushwhacked? That would only hurt himself and his plan, whatever that was. By golly, they'd come within a whisker of catching him off his guard up there in the girl's room. Who? And damn it—why?

All of this was running through his mind as he swiftly saddled up and hit the trail out of town. Somehow there was no pursuit. And this too surprised him. He had figured that whoever was after him would try to cut him off at the livery when he went for his horse, or they might be along the trail. At any rate, he rode out of town quickly, but with all necessary caution.

He had taken the south trail out of town, which led to his herd of longhorns and his Texas cowboys, but he didn't go far along it before turning off and changing direction. To make doubly sure of losing his tracks, he rode his spotted pony into a creek and over rocks and hard ground where there would be no chance of even the sharpest tracker cutting his trail. Then, when he was sure nobody was following, he changed direction again and came in toward the cattle from the east. Except that he didn't ride into camp. He found a good place in a stand of cottonwoods where he had protection both visually and from the point of view of sound. He would be able to hear even the finest tracker coming through the dry underbrush, especially at night. Here he picketed his horse and, and a good distance away, threw his bedroll.

Overhead the sky was clear. Light came from the bright new moon that had just risen. He could see, he could hear, and he could smell.

Now he had to think. The only possibility he came up with was that Rumpel must have competitors—one, maybe more—in what he was attempting. And it was beginning to be clear to Slocum what the pudgy man wanted.

If Rumpel was working with Gallup, he was onto something bigger than cattle shipments. Gallup was no fool, nor was he any small potato in the Army brass. Slocum had heard of Fabio Gallup. Galloping Gallup, the name was, still ringing from his fight with Pickett and a couple of other memorable moments during the War Between the States, not to mention the fact that he had shown his mettle against the Sioux. Why a man with a career as successful as Gallup's would wish to associate with a man like Rumpel was a mystery. Unless . . . unless, but of course! Could it not be that Rumpel had something on the colonel? In a way, wasn't that how he'd been hooked to drive the herd north? Hell, damn near

everyone had something in his past that could be
used against him by a man as adroit as Rumpel.

Suppose that was the case? What would Rumpel
be after? Why would he want to use an Army colonel
in his scheme? What could a man like Gallup do for
a man like Ralph Rumpel?

Guns? No, that wasn't likely. But Gallup was the
commanding officer at Fort Tyson, which was still in
the process of being built. And Fort Tyson meant
Indians. The Sioux. And the Sioux meant . . .?

Here he could go no further. Words like "gold,"
"silver," "mining," "railroad" drifted into his
thoughts, but none of them hooked up with anything.

At the same time, if Gallup was indeed working
with Rumpel, why would he have told Magic Otto to
treat him well unless he was considered by the colonel to be an ally? It just didn't make sense that anyone connected with either Gallup or Rumpel—and
especially Rumpel—would want to drygulch him or
do him physical harm in any way. But then, what
sense did it make for Rumpel to risk losing three
thousand head of Longhorns by sending them into
Falling Lance country?

That left Rudabaugh. And—wait a minute! Rumpel had mentioned Boyd Flanagan! Yes. He had told
him that Flanagan wasn't working with him, or
rather, vice versa, that he, Rumpel wasn't in with
Flanagan. No matter. Rumpel had made a point of
mentioning Flanagan and at the same time had emphasized that he had nothing to do with the man.
Slocum remembered now that the words Rumpel had
used had been spoken much in the way of a threat.
There was the sound, the atmosphere of threat or a

warning in them. Why? What had Rumpel really been saying? And what of the Fort Worth Vigilance Committee? It was—or so it had seemed at the time —mainly with them that he had run afoul down in Texas. Rumpel had claimed only to be an agreeable influence with them; and he had also implied that Boyd Flanagan was the leader.

Yes—Flanagan. He tried to think back now to what he knew about Flanagan. The man had ridden with Bloody Bill Anderson during the war, and also with one of the renegade border gangs after the peace had been signed. Suddenly he thought of the gang that had stopped the herd on the Sedalia trail. Had that been Flanagan's bunch? And had that been part of Rumpel's plan?

But his thoughts suddenly snapped off when he caught the new smell that came into the air. And he was instantly on guard, slipping away from where he had been sitting cross-legged with his back to a tree, unsnapping the leather thong that held his cross-draw handgun in its holster, and feeling down to the throwing knife tied against his leg. That smell was strong, sharp, pungent, filling the night air, almost overcoming it. Yet there was no question to Slocum's trained nose that it was Indian. And more than likely Sioux.

Whatever tribe didn't matter. The man was there, close. And it could be there were others nearby. Slocum wondered if he or they had just happened to cut his trail, or whether they were part of whoever had tried to drygulch him in Antelope. It didn't matter— at least not now. What concerned him now was the simple fact of survival. Who and how many was he up against? As always, in the cutting moment when one faced the high possibility of death, the only question was life.

Colonel Fabio Gallup, commanding officer of Fort Tyson, had just uncorked a fine bottle of sherry and poured into the two glasses. Liberally. There was the fine nutty odor of quality rising from the glass he handed his visitor, and with his next gesture he lifted his own glass and sniffed. "God bless us all—that is an excellent sherry. Excellent! Even if I say so myself." And his rather stiff face broke into a web of lines and creases to indicate to Ralph Rumpel that the man also had his human side and wasn't all spit, polish, leather, and cold steel.

They were seated in the colonel's office, facing each other across their mahogany-colored drinks.

"You risked it coming all the way up here, Rumpel. And we can drink to that, man."

A smile colored Ralph Rumpel's puffy cheeks as he raised his glass. "Here's to our enterprise," he said warmly, and smacked his lips as he took a sip of the sherry. "I don't know sherry much. Whiskey's my drink. But this is damn good. I must say it is damn good!"

The colonel now offered a cigar from the silver box on his desk. "You'll find this damn good too, Rumpel." And he took one himself, rolled it between his fingers, testing its pliability, then held it under his nose for aroma, and finally bit out the little bullet at one end. Then he put the cigar in his mouth and turned it, getting the end good and wet. Finally, he struck a lucifer, let the sulphur burn off, and then bending his head he lighted the cigar. Leaning forward, he blew out a small pillow of smoke, then leaned back in his chair and drew again; and this time he emitted a large cloud that rose slowly toward the ceiling of his office.

Rumpel, delighted at the hospitality, followed suit. The room was soon filled with the delightful aroma of pure Havana tobacco.

Rumpel inspected the finely even ash forming on the end of his cigar. He cocked an eye at his host. "Same source?"

The colonel nodded.

"But not the sherry."

"Not the sherry. The sherry came from San Francisco. I always have a case or two on hand."

Rumpel knew full well that the colonel's salary did not in any way permit such a luxury, but he made no comment, of course, simply registering the interesting observation in his already well-stocked mind.

Another appreciative moment passed, during which the two men—the short, pudgy one, and the tall, whip-lean, wholly military gentleman—addressed themselves to those two finer products of man's ingenuity.

Then Fabio Gallup cleared his throat. "You see, Rumpel, of course one must expect officialdom— and especially the military—to move at a ponderous gait. After all, it's self-protective in a way."

"Protective of the brass, I'd wager," Rumpel put in tartly.

Gallup offered this remark a withering look, all the way down his long nose. "Mebbe. But principally, it's simply the fact of size and complexity, not to forget differences of human type. And my point is that one sometimes has to move in a more direct, and certainly a quicker fashion. After all, you can't stand around picking your nose when there's a prairie fire and some damn fool insists on going through channels."

"For sure, for sure," Rumpel agreed warmly.

"It was of course an idiotic, stupid thing that happened in Antelope." Fabio Gallup cleared his throat as he warmed to the subject that had been bothering him for a few days now. "And I'm glad you're here, Rumpel, to see what you can do about it. I mean, something has to be done. Something has got to be done about it."

"Sure," Rumpel said, smooth as silk. "Sure."

"That fool Rudabaugh went berserk, tried to mop up one of the saloons—Matt Otto's place—and made the damn mistake of targeting Slocum."

"To his dismay, I have heard," Rumpel said ruefully. "Yes, I have details on the stupid affair; one of the reasons for my visit."

"I'm frankly glad to see you, Rumpel. We need to talk, and not just about Rudabaugh. Which, I understand, began over a woman."

Rumpel suddenly laughed. "Of course. But of course. Is there any other kind of trouble?"

And together they chuckled over that sage remark.

Ralph Rumpel was pleased. He was in fact enjoying himself. He always did enjoy it when things began to work out. For instance, here was Gallup playing right along with it. And Slocum was proving to be just the man he wanted for this particular job. "Gallup, I'm glad about the action with Rudabaugh.

It proves Slocum is the man for the job."

"For trailherding three thousand head of longhorn cattle from Texas to Montana?"

"And, uh, possibly other things," Rumpel replied in a careful tone of voice, his eyes fully on his companion.

"I see."

"And it also ties him in more with us in a certain way. Of course, providing he passes the test."

"Test?"

"Yes. If he proves to be all he's touted to be, then maybe we—I—might have a use for him."

Rumpel's switch from the plural to the singular pronoun was not lost on Fabio Gallup, but he held his tongue, looking now with disdain on the other man.

Then Gallup said, "How do you figure that? The man could easily have gotten himself killed."

Rumpel was grinning. "On the contrary, Colonel. Rudabaugh and his bunch were the lucky ones. You know, they also tangled in Fort Worth, and Slocum whipped his ass then, too."

Fabio Gallup raised his index finger in acknowledgment. "True. It is true. He's a good man. I spoke hastily."

"But—he is a dangerous man," said Ralph Rumpel. A button on his vest had popped open, and he saw the colonel's eyes looking there. "Just the sort we need," he said as his hand reached to close the offending gap in his clothing. Then, without even a thought about it, he swiftly checked his fly.

Gallup watched him with sharp pleasure, enjoying fully his own superiority in being lean. "You understand, Rumpel, it's not been easy here. I mean, I'm on view a good deal, I hope you realize."

"Oh, I do. And that is precisely what I am counting on, Fabio. Your position, your reputation, and your, uh, loyalty to our . . . to the cause." He grinned gently into the atmosphere, as though his thoughts were miles away, dreaming pleasantly. They weren't. They were right on top of that United States Army officer seated in front of him and who was proving to be one of the most useful individuals he had ever manipulated.

Rumpel had Gallup by—as he put it to himself— the gonads. But he didn't squeeze. He was careful with the man. True, Gallup was a military man, and therefore, in Rumpel's opinion, not very bright; except that Gallup had a streak of something in him that was "different" from the customary military officer. Somehow the man could not so easily be pushed, handled, manipulated. Rumpel wasn't sure just what it was, but he did want to know. He would have given a lot to know. But he could wait. He was a patient man, and in his kind of work patience always paid off. Meanwhile, since he did have the drop on Gallup, he could use his front—as Army colonel— to good advantage.

"As you know, Fabio, I am counting on you to stamp out the whiskey trains that have been all but overrunning the country."

"I have a full detail on the job, Rumpel, including Slocum keeping his ear to the ground for me. But we have of course been hampered by the fact that men need to be deployed toward the Indian situation. You understand, I am sure."

Rumpel inclined his head in hesitant agreement. "We must get at the problem right away, Colonel."

"I understand. And as I have already told you . . ." Gallup opened his hands and gazed at the top of his companion's head.

Rumpel was silent, obvious disapproval masking his face. Gallup read the signs and he was not disturbed. Rumpel knew the situation very well, only of course he couldn't let on that he knew. The man was sometimes quite stupid, Gallup decided.

"How long will you be staying, Ralph?" Gallup now asked, intentionally resorting to familiarity in order to maintain his own position, which Rumpel was always trying to erode. "You're of course fully welcome for as long as you wish to stay, though if it's for any length of time I shall have to have a reason for your visit." And then he added, "To be sure, the whiskey train business could be reason enough. A concerned citizen, etcetera, trying to do something for the communal good, and so forth."

Rumpel's smile was tight as he felt Gallup trying to manipulate him. The fool! "Only a day or two," he said coolly. "My principal purpose has been to check on Slocum, and of course how our operation in general was getting on."

"As I see it, a man like Slocum can be helpful, no doubt about it. On the other hand, he could be a real pain in the ass to us."

"But it's those pain-in-the-ass people who can give an operation the vinegar that's needed."

Gallup had to agree with that. He in fact chuckled. "Yeah, indeed. Nothing like a dose of vinegar up the cat's old rooty-tooty, eh?"

He fell silent, leaning back a little, remembering his military bearing, and at the same time thinking of when he might be free of his debt to Rumpel. He had always liked the action, that was true. The excitement. But there was also the risk. He didn't always like that. Still, damn it, by God, he was an officer in the United States Army. A colonel, Goddamn it! And as such he was a whole hell of a lot more than that potbellied, spongy, fat-assed, mushy little bugger sitting there thinking his shit didn't stink.

But Rumpel was speaking. "Has Slocum started to move the herd yet?"

"I haven't heard yet, but I expect to hourly."

"And there were no repercussions about Rudabaugh?"

"As I understand it, only with the girl. Rudabaugh, or some of his men, one or more—I don't know the details yet—anyway, she was roughed up, beaten. And so the law is involved. Not the Army, of course, though we are often expected to cooperate with civilian law. With the town marshal, for instance, at Antelope."

"And who is that? Is it anyone we know, someone we can use?"

The colonel was shaking his head from side to side even before Rumpel finished speaking. "It is a man named Roller."

"Roller? I don't know the name."

"Remember it," Gallup said, glad for the opportunity to be ahead of Rumpel. "Clarence Roller is a tough boy."

"I take it that you mean he can't be bought."

"I do."

A grin came swiftly into Rumpel's doughy face, but there was no humor in it. "My friend, there isn't a man alive who can't be bought. That includes lawmen, judges, politicians, and, uh, I do believe, Army officers." And with delight he watched the flush sweep over Fabio Gallup's face.

After a pause, during which Gallup poured another drink, Rumpel said, "So Slocum has got all his wagons, his oxen and drivers, and his Remingtons."

The colonel nodded.

"Good, then. I have a good picture. It's not quite the way we set it up, though I did count on his not following the Sedalia for too long. The boys helped me there." Rumpel rubbed his chin. "The boys can be persuasive." He stood up. "No, I am glad Slocum decided to throw the herd this way toward Cold Rock. He had little choice, after all, and I was counting on him to be bold. But also that he would feel that he had made the decision to come this route."

Both men were standing now, and they finished their drinks, nodding a silent toast to their joint enterprise.

"I'll be pulling out for Antelope in the morning," Rumpel said.

"I'll send an escort with you part of the way," Gallup replied.

"I appreciate it, Colonel."

"Army regulations," Gallup said.

"Still—thank you, Colonel."

And as Rumpel left his office Fabio Gallup felt the knot in the pit of his stomach. He was feeling that knot more and more lately. And right now the way

Rumpel's tone of voice was when he addressed him as "Colonel" brought it on even stronger. For Fabio Gallup knew that in no way would he be able to face a court-martial. He just couldn't, that was all. He just could not.

He lay as flat as he could, sealed to the earth, the cool night-grass fragrant in his nostrils. With one leg drawn up and his boot toe dug in for swift movement, he let his muscles relax. Yet Slocum was also in a trigger state of tension so that he could charge on the instant.

He was holding his Arkansas throwing knife in one hand; his handgun was still in its holster. With the possibility of more attackers being present, a shot would be ruinous. The blade was always silent, sure in its secrecy—provided the other didn't cry out. Loose, relaxing against the tension that kept coming in like little waves, he knew that wonderful feeling that he was "just right."

No sound came from the thick foliage before him, but all at once the Indian was in front of him, clearly outlined in the moonlight. Not a big man, but lean, obviously powerful. His body touched the leaves along the edge of the brush yet without making a sound as he moved. Evidently he was studying the terrain carefully, listening for the slightest sound that would indicate Slocum's presence. In his hand he carried a bow, along with an arrow for shooting.

Slocum didn't need any second thought to remind him how swiftly that arrow could be fired. He had seen the Sioux in action often enough to know their ability. He lay absolutely still, breathing carefully, his eyes on the warrior, yet while his look was keen, it wasn't tight. His whole body was in that special balance between tension and relaxation where he could spring on the instant from a stillness to the swiftest action. The Indian was very close. He would either come right on him or he would find a sign and might move on, pretending to look elsewhere, only to surprise Slocum later. It was an old trick, but one that had cost a lot of lives.

Slocum knew full well that he had one chance—his ambush. The moment the Indian came in front of him he'd kill him. But absolute silence was demanded. There was no way for Slocum to know how many others might be in the surrounding foliage and trees.

The whole of the action had to take place in less than a second, and with no sound. The knife would have to do its business on the first stroke. For to engage in a prolonged battle would only attract any other hostiles who might be present.

The Sioux was being very careful. It was obvious to Slocum that he had seen warfare. He could tell that by the way the man moved. There was confidence in him, the confidence of a warrior who had tasted victory.

The warrior was crouched now, staring about, listening, sniffing. Slocum could see that there was something that was making him suspicious.

The Indian took a step forward. Slocum could smell him more strongly now, and he knew the Indian could smell him. He was still moving with extreme care, indicating to Slocum that he knew the white man was there, somewhere near, though Slo-

cum was certain the Indian couldn't see him. When
he moved, the grass whispered, as though moved by
the air. He was wearing a breechclout, and while
Slocum could make out the bow and quiver with
arrows, he knew there had to be a hunting knife.

Slocum drew in a breath, and let it out slowly,
carefully, to empty himself. Then, in a long leap, he
shot up from the earth. The Indian felt it almost before it happened, warned by some tiny sound or pre-
monition, and he wheeled with the speed of a
mountain cat. Slocum was too close for him to use
the bow and arrow, and the Sioux let go of them and
lost time in grabbing at his knife. Slocum struck with
his throwing knife and caught his opponent in the
shoulder, following up with his left fist catching the
Indian in the temple and staggering him. Instantly he
struck again, this time at the Indian's body. But the
man was fast and received only a thin cut across his
ribs. And now he had his own knife out of its sheath.

Slocum struck again, this time for the Indian's
windpipe, and as the man thrust with his knife in
return, he sliced into his belly, entering just below
the ribs and going in to the hilt.

For a moment there was a struggle. The Indian
was tough. Slocum leaned into the blade, trying to
push it upward toward the lungs and heart. But the
man wouldn't give in. Finally, Slocum pulled the
blade out and struck again, and then again. The body
tightened under the blows. Then it relaxed.

For a while Slocum lay still, listening for sounds
of any approaching companions of the Sioux. Finally, he withdrew his knife, wiped it on the grass,
and slipped it back into its sheath.

He listened for sounds of anything unusual. Had the Indian been alone? Had he come upon Slocum's horse, picketed a good distance away but easy enough to come upon by a good tracker, whose sense of smell alone would have discovered the animal? Slocum went carefully through the trees and found his spotted pony picketed just where he had left him. It was still dark and so he couldn't usefully search for tracks that the Sioux might have made.

And yet at the same time there was something nagging at him. Why hadn't the Sioux found his horse? Or had he? Slocum somehow had the feeling that he hadn't. And it was still too dark to check for signs. Still, he had that hunch. And that was part of the "something" that was bothering him.

Carefully he slipped back to where he had left the dead warrior, moving with extreme care for fear of company. The question that was occupying him now was whether the Indian had been following him or whether he had more or less stumbled on the cattle herd and his own trail. He leaned toward the latter notion, but he still wasn't absolutely sure.

But there was still something else, something unsatisfied in his recapitulation of his fight with the Indian. Well, he decided, he'd done enough thinking on it, and, characteristically, he simply let the matter drop. The night was clear, and looking up at the starry sky he could see that it was past midnight. It would soon be dawn. Finding a new place for cover, he threw his bedroll onto some pine needles and was soon asleep.

The sun was just coming up when he awakened. He went quickly to where his pony was standing and looking into the distance. When he saw Slocum approaching he snorted, then shook his head, his mane flying about.

Slocum could find no sign that the Indian had been anywhere near his horse, and as he walked back to where the dead man lay, the feeling he'd had right after the fight came back to him—that there was something strange about the whole action. He took time now to see if there was any sign of other Sioux nearby, but he found nothing. It was clear then that the man who had tried to kill him had indeed been alone. For if he had been with others, they had certainly not waited around but had gone off and left him. Which would have been most unlikely.

He had stopped and was standing beside a big cottonwood tree, studying the scene around him, when he heard a slight movement in the brush. Quickly he faded back, alert to sound, smell, the slightest appearance of anything unusual. Under cover, he waited. Then he heard the sound again.

It was a horse, walking through the brush. When it came into the little clearing in front of Slocum, he saw that it was a dun pony, carrying a low-canteled roping saddle, with a brand on its left shoulder which Slocum couldn't read at that distance. It had to be the Indian's horse, except that no Indian would be riding a saddle like that.

And then he knew what it was that had been bothering him. Strange, how he hadn't stumbled on it during the fight, but of course all his attention had been on the fight itself. In a few moments he had walked to where the dead man lay. He reached down and turned the man over. No, he was no Indian, even though he was dressed like one, with a breechclout and moccasins. But he wasn't all white, either. A breed. Half Indian, half white, though leaning on the side of the Indian more than the white.

Yet he had acted, fought, smelled absolutely like an Indian. He had fought a hard fight, had behaved well as he had approached the place where Slocum had been hidden. A white man wouldn't have been as capable as this man had been. He was for sure no greener, no miner or sodbuster or even a cowpoke. Only not white either. For in his action, Slocum placed the Indian in him as dominant.

The point was an important one, for it indicated that he was—or had been—a lone wolf. There wouldn't have been any warriors riding with him, and he had not stumbled onto Slocum's trail. He had been intentionally tracking him. This was absolutely clear.

But why?

5

In a back room of the Fancy Eatery in Antelope, the short, dumpy man with the fat cigar and the two gold rings on his fingers stared relentlessly at a disheveled and furious Link Rudabaugh.

"So your man got himself killed," Ralph Rumpel was saying. His words fell hard and cold into the room, as though they were being read from a gravestone. He spat at a spittoon near his foot and missed completely, splattering the wooden floor. He watched with a certain satisfaction as Rudabaugh's eyes darted to the action, while at the same time he went right on smoking, paying no attention whatever to his inferior aim. It was his job to spit, after all, someone else's to clean up.

"The sonofabitch didn't follow orders, was the trouble."

Rumpel's round head was revolving in a sign of total negation, turning as far as it could go from one side to the other. "No." The small word popped out of his mouth as though he was spitting out a seed from a piece of fruit. "No," he repeated, spitting it this time like a bullet. "It was you. You shouldn't have told him to follow a man like Slocum in the first place. Especially without asking me first."

Rudabaugh remained silent, though sucking his teeth noisily. Then he said, "The bastard was lucky. I'll get him next time."

Rumpel was again shaking his head. "No! There will be no next time. At least not until my business with you is finished. From now on, Rudabaugh, you will follow orders. That means that you will do only what you are told. I will be very clear in what I tell you. Because one mistake can ruin my whole plan. And that simply must not happen!"

Rudabaugh glowered but said nothing.

"Do you get me?"

"I do."

Rumpel drew on his cigar and then released a cloud of smoke in the direction of the ceiling, though some of it wafted in the other man's direction. He took the cigar out of his mouth. "I want you to get on up to Cold Rock. I've got a message I want you to deliver." He reached inside his black frock coat and drew out an envelope. He held it in his hand, as though feeling its weight. "You hand this to a man named Kinsolving. Hector Kinsolving. You do not give it to anybody else. Only Kinsolving. Personal. You understand?"

"I do."

Rumpel studied the scar over Rudabaugh's left eye. "I will not accept any mistake. This is important."

"Where do I find this feller Kingsolvis?"

"Kinsolving! Say it!"

"Kinsolvin'."

"Say it again! Kin . . . solv . . . ing!"

"Aw shit!"

"Say the name, Rudabaugh, or your ass is in more trouble than you can handle. And you know that, by God!"

"Kinsolving. Kinsolving. Kinsolving! Where do I find the sonofabitch!"

Rumpel got to his feet, his cigar clamped in his teeth, ash falling over his vest, to which he paid no attention. He took the cigar out of his mouth and said, "He will find you."

The spotted pony was keeping a good pace without Slocum having to urge him. He was traveling through tall grass, a good three feet high, and there was a profusion of wild fruits—strawberries, cherries, currants, grapes, and gooseberries. Without any order from Slocum the spotted pony began to lope through the low hills bordering one bank of the river, which was lined with good timber. And then all at once he knew that someone was on his trail.

He drew rein and sat absolutely still in his saddle, listening. Now there was nothing. Whoever it was behind him was a good tracker. Indian? There was one way to find out. He kicked the spotted horse into a canter and then into a gallop, heading away from the river toward a tableland around which there would be good cover, and he hoped a place where he could find some elevation.

The horse had picked up on his need to move swiftly, and in only moments they had reached a thick line of cottonwoods and box elders. Seeing an opening that wasn't that much of a trail, Slocum marked it in his mind and rode on. Several yards beyond there was another opening, and he drew rein and walked his horse into the cover of the trees. He dismounted and led the animal through the trees back to the place he had noted when he'd ridden past just before.

In a few moments he heard the rider coming slowly down the trail, obviously being careful and checking the tracks left by Slocum's spotted horse. There was something familiar about him, even though his face was turned away, and Slocum felt he must have seen him before, though he couldn't place him. Then horse and rider had passed.

Slocum led the spotted pony out of the trees, mounted quickly, and slowly he began trailing the man who had been trailing him.

The action had all happened so simply, so easily, and in certain details so unexpectedly well that no one could have imagined it taking place in such a fashion. In other words, all went smoothly and according to plan. Most unusual.

The day was extremely warm. Slowly the mule-drawn wagon moved across the floor of the great valley. It was a big wagon, and it was loaded heavily with barrels and crates packed with bottles. The barrels were destined for various sutler stores in the territory, the bottles for the more private consumption of the officers of the Army of the West in residence at the various forts and military outposts.

A pair of quite aged men sat on the wagon box seat directly behind the mules, while a third man, also of historic years, rode a spavined old crowbait of a horse just a short distance ahead of this treasured and highly valuable cargo. From above, a white-hot sun beat down indiscriminately on men and animals.

"Fixin' to be a short spring," said the oldster holding the leather lines of the mule team.

His companion muttered through dry lips, "Nature don't never show favorites, either the sour or the sweet of it bein' all the same to 'er, by God." And nodded his aged head, which was covered by a beaten-up Stetson hat with a bite taken out of its brim—likely by a pack rat. His tobacco-streaked gray beard quivered as he spat with sudden swiftness onto the rump of one of the mules. "Could favor a drink, by Jesus! Hotter'n a firecracker on the Fourth, by God it is!"

The mules bobbed their heads with each step as they advanced across the burning prairie. The pair on the wagon box dozed.

Three-Fingers Barney Loop, riding the gray crow-bait, turned back toward the wagon. "Creek up yonder," he announced, canting his head in the direction of a line of cottonwoods, which the two on the wagon box had already noted.

"Good place to give us a rest an' let the animals blow," the driver said. His name was Clancy O'Rourke. He turned to his dozing companion. "Wake up, Ollie. We're just coming into Falling Lance country."

"Better let go yer cock and grab yer scalp," Ollie said, lifting his eyelids as though they weighed a ton.

"Hot," Clancy said.

"It's all there is out in this goddamn place," Oliver Wirehouse said. "Nothin' out here 'ceptin' the goddamn weather."

"An' the goddamn godless Injuns, don't forget!" Three-Fingers Barney Loop said, his words gloomy with warning.

Meanwhile, Clancy O'Rourke, the driver, also spat at the rump of the nearest mule, but his aim was not as accurate as Ollie's, the brown and yellow tobacco spittle falling onto the singletree behind his target.

Silent now under the demands of caution, the three veterans of the hard life warily approached the creek. All carried weapons—sidearms and Winchesters—and were in fact old hands at hauling whiskey and other important liquids from the Union Pacific tracks, just south of Miller's Crossing, and on up to the pass in the Little Rim Range that led north to Cold Rock by way of Antelope. There had been various troublesome encounters with the Sioux and others from time to time, but thus far nothing too serious, the natives showing discretion in the face of the approaching sea of white men. Though at the same time, when there was opportunity, the red men attacked with tremendous effect, taking advantage of certain small groupings of whites whenever possible. For the most part the whites were proving more and more numerous and thus overwhelming.

As far as the whiskey men were concerned, they had managed on not a few occasions to pay off the hostiles with a bottle or two of the firewater. In a certain way, a tenuous working relationship had been worked out between the whiskey peddlers and certain of the Arapahos, Shoshones, and Sioux.

"We'll make it to Antelope pretty directly, come nightfall," Three-Fingers Barney predicted, breathing heavily. "We could handle a break, I reckon." His breath whistled as he spoke, and after finishing what he had to say, his chest pumped, and he looked as though he was in pain. He was, though not badly, having received a bullet close to his lungs some years back, courtesy of some Comanches.

"If you can handle that ringtailed bronc you're forkin' there," Clancy O'Rourke said, winking as he drove a sharp elbow into the ribs of Ollie Wirehouse, who let out a gasp of pain, followed by curses.

Shortly, seated in the shade, the three old buzzards tucked into some jerked beef, hardtack, canned peaches, and liberal servings of their own merchandise.

Three-Fingers brought out a deck of cards, and while they were finishing off their repast with some of the product they were transporting, they played a few hands of stud. They were in good fettle when they started up again.

"We're gonna make Antelope pretty directly," Clancy said. Clancy had been a sergeant in the Army some years ago, and after his discharge as a result of wounds received in combat with the Kiowa down in Texas, he'd taken on as sutler at an Army post on the high plains of Wyoming. His experience in that field had proven useful to the present enterprise.

Scratching his beard now, Clancy squinted at the sun, then looked over at Three-Fingers, who was mounting his horse. But he didn't really take in the horse and rider he was looking at, for at that very moment a cry escaped Ollie Wirehouse, who was suddenly sitting bolt upright in the wagon box, his jaw hanging down as far as it would go.

His companions were staring with him now at the seven near-naked Indian riders who were approaching, their leader's hand raised in the sign of peace.

"Jesus H. Christ," whistled Three-Fingers. "Jesus H. Christ!"

Shaking just a mite, Clancy O'Rourke now raised his hand also in the sign of peace.

"Jesus ain't gonna help us now," Ollie said.

"Take it slow," Clancy said. "Don't forget we got the whiskey. Somethin' tells me that'll be what they is after."

Slocum had followed the rider who was tracking him for only a short distance. He knew that the man ahead would swiftly discover that he had lost the trail and would turn around and come back to find it. Quickly he hid his horse and climbed a tall cottonwood with a branch overhanging the trail. Crouching on the branch above the trail he had just left, Slocum settled himself firmly, hoping that his pony would be silent in the dry brush where he'd concealed him.

He had only just made it back to the tree and climbed up to the overhanging branch when he heard the rider coming. It was an old ruse he was pulling, and he hoped it would work. Sometimes the oldest and most familiar tricks were the best. He was working on the assumption that no one would figure somebody would try to pull such an old one out of the bag.

Now as the rider approached along the trail below him, Slocum readied himself as his eyes took in the man's figure. He couldn't see his face beneath the wide hat brim, but he took note of the great amount of hair on the backs of his fingers, which were holding his pony's reins.

Slocum was perfectly balanced on the branch, and now he drew his six-gun carefully. There was still something he found familiar in the man's appearance. What was it? His attitude, perhaps. He didn't seem the average cowpoke nor the gunswift type either. Yet there was something about the man that meant he was no one to mess with.

The rider had just ridden past the branch and now had his back to Slocum.

"Hold it right there," Slocum said quietly.

The rider didn't hesitate but drew rein immediately, raising his free hand—his gun hand—up level with his shoulder. His horse, a strawberry roan, snorted and spooked a little, and the rider muttered something to quiet him.

Slocum suddenly dropped to the trail, his six-gun in his hand. The roan spooked again just a little, but the man again calmed the animal with his voice. Then Slocum realized it was the man he'd met at Magic Otto's Lead Dollar Saloon in Antelope, the man who'd said his name was Roller.

Roller had turned his horse now, lowering his hand a little.

"Unbuckle," Slocum said. "Carefully."

And carefully the man with the stonelike face with all its deeply cut lines unbuckled his gunbelt and tossed it onto the ground at Slocum's feet. "You left your horse up in the tree, did you? Excepting I see you sent him on down the trail. Dumb, huh? Falling for that old turkey. Well, that's why you're holding that shooter and I'm looking at it."

"Climb on down," Slocum said. "Your name's Roller, is it?"

"That's what I told you back in the Lead Dollar."

"That doesn't answer my question," Slocum said.

"Roller," his prisoner said. "Clarence Roller. Was and is."

Slocum eyed him carefully. "Why are you following me?"

"I want to talk to you."

"Why didn't you talk back at Antelope?"

"You will recollect, Slocum, that your departure from the Lead Dollar was kind of fast—and even unexpected."

"That is so. Well, then, talk now."

Slocum quickly holstered his gun, then stepped over and plucked Roller's six-shooter out of its gunbelt, broke it, and emptied the shells into his hand. "Good enough," he said. "We'll pick up my pony and then we'll talk." And he tossed Roller's reholstered Smith & Wesson to him, keeping the shells, however.

The game had opened fast and high, with the betting crisp, the three old-timers settling right in with four of the Indians while the remaining three watched.

It was the shank of the day, the sky a rich, singing blue. And though it was hot there by the thin little creek, now and then came a stirring of a light breeze, which brought just the right comfort for the game that was in progress. They had set up by a small clearing in the willows that lined the little creek. Yet the players—at any rate the three oldsters—were not especially aware of the pastoral setting. Theirs was a grim attention to the business at hand. It could safely be said that all the players, red and white, were enjoying themselves.

"Injuns, they surely go for the gambling," Three-Fingers Barney Loop had sagely observed when the one who was apparently the leader had produced the worn deck of cards. It was a deck even older and greasier than the one the trio had been playing with.

The red men spoke very little, even among themselves, and their designated leader handled English haltingly, using signs to help convey his meaning. He managed to get it across to the three white men that they had seen the three playing cards at one of their stops and so had followed them with the hope of joining them in a game.

The three, however, were not fooled by this attempted diversionary comment. Clancy O'Rourke had been the first to point out—from the side of his mouth—that they were obviously after the whiskey; it was easy enough to smell it. And his two companions were swift to see the problem. The sensible move, at least for the moment, was acceptance of the inevitable.

"Shit!" Ollie Wirehouse had muttered, talking down along his shirtfront so that the Indians wouldn't be so apt to hear what he was saying, "Shit! For a minute I'd thought they was maybe our delivery contact. But it don't look like it."

"Just so long as it ain't St. Peter's our contact," muttered Three-Fingers Barney.

"Far as I reckoned it, it's a feller name of Clyde

Hooligan, an' he's supposed to meet up with us at Pine Gap."

"By God, we're almost at the Gap right now," Three-Fingers muttered, speaking into his handful of cards.

"Then where in hell is he?" Ollie Wirehouse wanted to know. "Ain't that a helluva note!"

Ollie had hardly gotten those words out of his mouth when they heard the horses blowing and stomping as they came into the clearing and swiftly spread out. There were a dozen horsemen, and as the cardplayers swiftly noted, all were heavily armed.

"It's Clyde Hooligan," Three-Fingers Barney said to his companions.

"You got it straight," the man on the big steel-dust gelding said. "An' you're the bunch Boyd Flanagan was expectin'." He suddenly drew the big hogleg at his right hip. It appeared in his hand before anyone of the players or Indians could react. Not that anyone might have. All took note of Clyde Hooligan's speed. None wished to verify his accuracy at that point.

"Tell them red devils to vamoose," Hooligan said. He was a narrow-shouldered man with big hands, and he had a sneer on his face.

"He sure ain't a man to argue with," Clancy O'Rourke muttered out of the side of his mouth to Ollie Wirehouse.

Ollie said nothing. He was standing with his mouth open.

Nor did the Indians say anything. One made an attempt to pick up his winnings, but a sound like a bark came from Clyde Hooligan and he changed his mind. Within the space of minutes the seven were gone.

"This the stuff?" Hooligan said, nodding toward the wagon.

"That's it." Clancy nodded. "Course we was told to turn it over to you."

"That you done," the man on the steel-dust gelding said. "There'll be a wagon here in a while, an' we can load 'er. You boys can skedaddle."

All at once the sound of gunfire broke into the clearing. The three old-timers cocked their heads toward where the sound was coming from.

Clyde Hooligan was grinning at their surprise. "That's just some of my boys showing them Injuns how their guns works."

"Shit," said Clancy O'Rourke. "Ain't that just a damn good way to get them Sioux all riled up again."

Hooligan's grin was even wider. "And ain't there the United States Army at Fort Reno and Tyson and all what's supposed to take care of us settlers and homesteaders and good, clean, honest citizens?"

Three-Fingers Barney looked grim at that. "Providin' the Army ain't already pinned down by a Injun feller named Falling Lance and God knows how many Sioux."

"Don't worry about it," Hooligan said, still grinning. "Somebody's already got that one figured."

Three-Fingers said nothing to that. First he looked at his two companions, Clancy and Ollie, and then he looked toward the top of the sky. "I just hope somebody knows what the hell he's doin'," he muttered sourly and spat in disgust, almost hitting his own boot but paying no mind to it. "This here caper's Flanagan's idea, far as I figure it, an' I just hope to God he knows what he's doing!" And he spat again, and before it even hit anything he was stomping off with his hands shoved deep in his pockets.

His two companions now mounted their horses, which they'd had tied to the back of the wagon carrying the whiskey. When they were out of earshot of Hooligan, Clancy looked in perplexity at Ollie. "D'you really think that horse's ass had them Injuns shot up? I can't believe what my ears was tellin' me!"

Ollie sniffed. "Might've just been throwing a scare into them," he said. "Whatever. By God, I wouldn't like much to have dealings with that feller, let me tell you."

"Hooligan?"

"Who'd you think I was talking about, fer Christ sakes?"

"Maybe Flanagan, I'd thought. Can't always tell what you're sayin'," Clancy said, and then belched loudly.

"We better get ourselves sobered up, my friend," Ollie pointed out. "This here event is getting somethin' all over the damn place. I will tell you, in no way do I have a mind to favor messin' with them damn Injuns."

"Let's haul ass," Clancy O'Rourke said. In another moment they had caught up with their friend Three-Fingers, and now the trio pulled themselves together somewhat.

"'Ceptin' I do wish one of you gents had had the

presence of mind to save some of that fine refreshment for us on our long journey," Clancy said.

Neither of his two companions said anything to that, and they rode on in silence.

The sky was darkening now, and the trio were beginning to feel not only the need for food but liquid support along with it. Presently, Clancy O'Rourke made the decision. "We can throw our camp yonder by the creek," he said. "We'll get goin' again early tomorrow."

It didn't take long to make camp, and when they were seated around their small fire, it was Three-Fingers who pulled a bottle out of his saddlebag, to the great and happy surprise of his companions. "Good thing somebody thinks ahead in this bunch," Three-Fingers said.

"I sure agrees with you, my lad," said Clancy O'Rourke, as he pulled a bottle of booze out of his bedroll and waved it at them.

It only remained for Ollie Wirehouse to top them by pulling two bottles from his warbag.

"Might last us through the night," Clancy said with a rich chuckle.

And his two companions agreed happily with this sage remark as they settled into the evening.

Shortly, after much exchange of banter and wild stories, not to mention happy speculations on the future, they began to grow sleepy.

In a little while the voices had stopped relating their fine stories, the heads had stopped nodding, and finally all that could be heard from the three rovers were the rich waves of snoring, each in a different key, swelling and subsiding and swelling again, while their horses also rested through the night with that patience such animals have toward their captors and masters, a patience that covered their lives and was sometimes appreciated by the men who made use of them.

6

He had been trying to bring the loose ends together, only there were so many loose ends. There was the scene with the four in his room at the Chip House in Fort Worth; and yes, even before that, the action with Link Rudabaugh at Jolly Burns's High Time. There had to be a connection. Then Rumpel and the threat of the vigilantes, and Boyd Flanagan. What was Rumpel up to? Why had he wanted him to drive three thousand longhorns north to Montana? And the Jayhawkers who'd stopped them on the Sedalia—did they have anything to do with Rumpel, either for or against him? Why had that dumpy little man with a brain like an Arkansas throwing knife wanted a herd driven north? It had all sounded a mite false at the time, and it still did: something made up to confuse. Rumpel as a cattle dealer had come off like a road agent in a church pulpit.

Those four idiots who'd braced him in the Chip House! And yet, Rumpel had seemed to have himself sized up pretty well. Did he know that the four would slop it up the way they did? And then the second action with Rudabaugh in Antelope, and the girl setting him up in her room. It all had the smell of something planned, arranged, and completely false. For it was clear that a man of Rumpel's obvious ability would never make such glaring mistakes as he had done. It was really as though the man had wanted things to go wrong. And now, finally, Roller. Who the hell was Roller, and what was he—if anything— to Rumpel? And yet, much as Slocum turned the situation over, he couldn't come up with a single piece of solid proof that anything was actually false. Except for his feeling about it. It just all smelled bad. He felt it, and his instinct knew it—that Rumpel was playing a game. He was a real possum, by God, throwing out a hot lead, followed by ice, then heat again. Slocum realized he was getting nowhere.

The trail now widened so that he could ride alongside Roller and his sorrel gelding. Neither of them had spoken since they'd mounted up after the confrontation where Slocum had gotten the drop on the lanky man. Slocum felt they had reached an understanding, that there was something between them in the way of a certain respect. But there was a lot to be explained. Who was Roller? Was he working on his own or was he a lawman? Or maybe a stock detective for the Association? Or working for Rumpel? Slocum remembered now that he'd also had these feelings and questions about Fabio Gallup. And Magic Otto.

The sun was halfway down the afternoon sky when they reached the herd. Slocum nodded to Turk, who was on the northern flank of the longhorns. "Anything?" he said, cutting his eye hard at the man who had been one of the four to brace him in the Chip House.

"Nothin' but the weather," Turk said, speaking

around a lucifer he was holding in his mouth as a toothpick.

Slocum watched to see if there was any recognition between Turk and Roller, but he saw nothing, felt nothing. They reached the cook wagon and Slocum drew rein. Beside him Roller followed suit. And when Slocum swung down from his saddle, Roller did the same.

Without a word, Slocum gave just a nod at the cook, a heavyset man named Loose-Lips Quinn, a bronc stomper of an earlier time, with more busted bones than hair on his scalp. Still without speaking, Slocum waited for coffee for himself and his guest.

Presently they were seated cross-legged in the lee of the cook wagon, facing the lowering sun and the orange light it was throwing over the vast stretch of prairie. Looking over at Loose-Lips Quinn, Slocum gave a slight nod for the man to disappear, which he did. Slocum watched him walking down toward the creek, limping a little, his right leg having been broken three times—not to mention ribs, an arm, and various other parts of his body—during the course of his career with the animal upon whom all who ventured more than a few yards out of any town relied upon completely. Horse thievery was the major crime, a fact which was painfully obvious to a number of those who had tried to defy it. And the bronc stomper was a key part of the education of the bronc into saddle-broke stuff. Slocum respected such men, knowing through experience what they went through, and knowing too how many of them, when their big days were over, were often cast aside, ending up swamping saloons, if lucky. Loose-Lips

Quinn was unusual. He reaped a high respect with the crew that Slocum was whipsawing.

"So talk," Slocum said, looking down at a piece of loose sage that was lying nearby. "I want to know why you were on my trail, Roller. You a bounty hunter? Far as I know I don't have a price on me."

Clarence Roller was squatting, sitting on his heels with his forearms on his thighs, his hands hanging down loose between the arch made by his legs. "Nope. I don't hunt men, Slocum. That's to say, I don't hunt 'em private like. Only when I'm with the law. Or maybe if it's a man needs to lie still and not move around so much. Like, he requires lying still —permanent. I'll help him get that permanent look then. But I take no pleasure in it."

"What are you doing on my tail, then?"

Roller didn't say anything to that. He took out a plug of tobacco from his shirt pocket and a clasp knife and cut off a good slice and popped it into his mouth and began chewing. His movements were deliberate, like he was following along with each one. Slocum had seen Indians move like that, and the man went up a notch or two in his estimation. He could see that in no way could this man be called slow; he just made his moves intentional. Surely he had to be not only fast but accurate with that Smith & Wesson. Slocum reached into his pocket and handed over the cartridges he'd taken.

"Obliged," Roller said, his cheek bulging as he shifted his chew so he could speak around it. "I ain't with the law, Slocum. And I ain't with the out-of-the-law neither. I don't mind hiring my gun, if the deal is right, and for sure the price. But generally, like as a rule, I got to satisfy what I am seeing in the situation."

"You're telling me you only kill the sonsof-bitches," Slocum said dryly.

Roller nodded. "I'd go along with that."

They were silent while two of Slocum's cowboys came up to the cook wagon for coffee. When they were gone again, Slocum took out a quirly, struck a wooden match with his thumbnail, one-handed, and lit up, canting his head against the flame. "So who you packing that hogleg for, Roller?"

Roller had been still squatting on his heels, and he remained so as he turned his head and let go a jet of saliva right into a wet pat of cow manure. His head raised just enough so he could squint at Slocum from beneath the wide brim of his Stetson hat.

"Why I'm packing that, I reckon, for the same feller you are, Slocum. Ralph Rumpel."

Colonel Fabio Gallup stood quietly by as one of the men loaded Ralph Rumpel's gear into the Army ambulance. Rumpel, smoking one of the colonel's cigars, also stood quietly until everything was ready.

"You'll be safe enough heading back south, Rumpel. And the lieutenant and his men have their orders."

"It's a damn pity I can't go the shortest possible route. Though I must say, I am not unhappy to follow your advice and take the long way around to Cold Rock."

Fabio Gallup found it extremely difficult at just that moment to control his face. Indeed, it wasn't merely his face that was itching so to break into a tremendous smile; his whole body tingled with the taste of victory as he turned to face his guest directly. "Not my advice,

Rumpel. I'm not offering advice. As the commanding officer here at Fort Tyson, I find it necessary to order you not to proceed directly north through Sioux country. My good man, I wouldn't allow the President of the United States to take that journey."

"I appreciate the comparison," Rumpel said. And Gallup again felt the pleasure coursing through him. Well, the dumpy little bastard had it coming to him.

"It does take you well out of your way, agreed," Gallup said smoothly. "But at least you'll get there. And, as I said, I am offering you an escort for part of the way. I hope you appreciate it and realize I am straining Army regulations, at least somewhat. Of course, I would do the same for another white man, Rumpel. Officially, you understand. I cannot show any favoritism. And indeed, I am not." His smile was tight, military, prepared for the lieutenant, the sergeant, and the men watching.

"I appreciate it, Fabio. And you will also appreciate my safe arrival, so that the success of my, uh, our plan can be assured."

"All ready, sir," the driver called.

"Good, Rumpel. Ralph. If you want one of the men to ride inside with you, just say so."

"That will not be necessary." Rumpel turned toward the ambulance. Then suddenly he turned back. "Oh, and don't forget, Gallup, keep your eyes and ears peeled for any news of that man I mentioned to you."

"Dunroodie? I'll send a message if I hear anything."

"Cotton Dunroodie," Rumpel added. "Of course, he might well be using an assumed name."

"Nothing new in that, is there?" said Gallup, unbending more, with the trace of a smile coming into his stern face.

"He's a slicker, that man," Rumpel said. "But as I told you, I have had it on very good authority that he might well show up in the territory."

"Well, you said you'd contacted the civilian law."

"I have. But you know, I want to cover everything. He's the kind of man who, if he got wind of our plan—even some part of it—could very well want to cause us trouble. He is really a snake." He looked thoughtfully into the middle distance. "I believe I could describe him as a sort of desperate snake." And with a wave of his hand he climbed up into the ambulance.

The colonel remained where he was as the driver cracked his whip and Rumpel and his escort took off. Cotton Dunroodie, he was thinking. Dunroodie. Somehow, somewhere he must have heard that name. For it rang something in him. Rumpel had made it very clear that he considered the man dangerous and a likely—not just a possible, but a likely—threat to the plan, should he get wind of it. And in fact, he had stressed the fact that Dunroodie never went anywhere in the country unless he was into something for his own advantage. Rumpel had brought up the name at the end of their meeting, and he had emphasized the need for Gallup to keep alert. But why such a man as he had described Dunroodie to be would want to come into this particular country, at this particular time, with the Sioux bristling and ready to hit the warpath, well, he'd not explained that at all.

The colonel put these thoughts out of his mind now as he reentered his quarters. It was still early morning, and a full day lay ahead. The work of building Fort Tyson was going ahead well. There was only one fly in the ointment, he told himself. Why couldn't the fort be named Fort Gallup?

Well, Rumpel had promised he would push for that when his plan bore fruit. Fabio Gallup was relying on that. He was relying on "Fort Gallup," and he was relying on the sealed lips of Ralph Rumpel in regard to that unfortunate matter of only a few years back. An affair that he had all but forgotten until that wretched little man had somehow dug it up and confronted him with it. No, Fabio Gallup, hero of the recent War Between the States, and especially at Pickett's Charge, could not, would never accept to be court-martialed. Never! It was unthinkable!

Slocum and Roller arrived at where the herd was being held only moments before the storm hit, and for a good hour the men were fighting to keep the cattle from stampeding. Fortunately the storm passed as swiftly as it had arrived. No damage was done, but it had exercised the entire crew, who had been getting restive at waiting so long. They had about worn out their welcome in Antelope, and some were even beginning to talk about their pay and when they were going to get it. One or two, more pushy than the rest, were asking where Slocum was and why didn't he push on to Cold Rock and pay them off.

Slocum was quick to pick up the negative attitude as soon as he and Roller rode in. He realized by now that Rumpel may well have encouraged it, or at least been counting on it. The man was playing his game high, fast, and hard. And it was obvious that the stakes were really big.

On a sudden impulse he mentioned it to Roller, as they were relaxing in one of Antelope's saloons following the near-stampede. "Do you figure his aim is just selling these cattle? I see three thousand head of Texas longhorns as a nice piece of money, but it ain't all that much. Why is this man putting on all this work, this trouble, all these men? Like us. Like Rudabaugh and the vigilante bunch. There has got to be more to it than just beef."

He had decided that the time had really come to force something—maybe from Rumpel. But shortly they would be in Cold Rock, and if he wasn't damn quick at sizing up the situation he could get caught with his pants down. He had a strong notion that Roller, who was certainly no dummy, was thinking along the same lines.

"I been thinking likewise," Roller said, his gray face looking even grayer than usual. "See, he hires you, then he hires me to watch you. Then who's he hiring to watch me? And like that." He wagged his head, shifting in his seat, his long fingers turning his glass of beer.

"There's talk of a new strike up at Cold Rock," Slocum said. "But not really public yet."

"I reckon not," Roller said wryly, looking around the crowded saloon. "Elsewise, this place would be emptier'n any old hole in the ground."

Slocum studied the man seated across from him. He had a good feeling about Roller. He had known the type. He would have bet the man had been a marshal or sheriff, and a good one. "You ever been with the law, Roller?"

It was then he caught the quick reflex in the other man's eyes.

"A while back," Roller said. And he looked down at the back of his hairy thumb, which was touching his near-empty glass of beer.

But Slocum had caught that sudden reaction. He knew something now, and he wondered whether Roller knew that he knew.

The ambulance rocked along the rutted trail that ran next to the telegraph poles crossing the rolling prairie. Overhead the sky was a deep blue, holding nothing in it except the white sun. Not even an eagle flew in it, nor even a wisp of cloud. The sky was naked and yet at the same time full, dancing with whatever it was composed of, dancing over the enormous prairie, the world above looking down at the world below.

On the prairie the ambulance was the only movement, a speck in the great wild sea of grass. Bouncing over the rutted trail, the ancient-looking conveyance carried no wounded, but one passenger, plus the Army driver, and a single armed escort whom Gallup had persuaded Rumpel to take at the last minute.

The driver, a pockmarked man of average stature in a faded blue uniform, kept the horses at a brisk pace. Nor did it appear to his passenger that he was making even the slightest effort to avoid bumps and holes in the trail.

The escort, seated beside the driver, had been placed there by Colonel Gallup solely for the protection of the passenger; he was not part of the regulation equipage. And while Rumpel had tried to refuse the man's presence, he had finally given in when Gallup had recounted to him details of a certain recent encounter between the soldiers and the Sioux at which the Army had come out second best.

An exceptionally wild lurch of the rattling conveyance almost threw the passenger right out of his seat, and he cursed magnificently. His choice of invective charmed the ears of both driver and escort.

"We should be there shortly, sir," the escort said.

Rumpel had regained his composure and now said, "How long do you reckon?"

The escort soldier turned his head slightly in acknowledgment of the question. "I'd say another twenty minutes to half an hour, sir." And he glanced at the driver for confirmation, but that man said nothing. His whole attention was either on his job or maybe far away in some dream.

Rumpel leaned forward, trying to watch the passing country. "I see the telegraph line is down," he said. "Indians, was it?"

"They're not sure," the escort said, half turning back toward the passenger. He was a corporal, Rumpel noted. "But they think it's likely the Sioux."

"I thought we were at peace with the Indians, Corporal."

"Yessir. But I'm sure you know how the hostiles are. You never know, is the point." And he flushed suddenly, evidently realizing he was getting tangled in his own words. "I mean, sir, one day it's peace, and the next it's all hell busted loose."

"I see," murmured Rumpel. And his short, puffy fingers felt inside his frock coat to make sure he had his derringer in place. And then he lapsed into silence.

With his eyes half closed, he contemplated his future moves. Thus far, all had gone well. Handling Slocum had been difficult, but he had chosen a good method. In fact, it was the method that he favored generally in any operation, which was to never let anyone know where the ace was. Three-card monte in actual daily action was how he liked to put it to himself.

Over the years he had developed it. And when he suddenly realized what an opportunity lay in the field of politics, he had, as it were, come into his own. Before that it had been gambling, bunco games, gold, silver, you name it. Building lots and the battle for the county seat when he was in Cimarron had led him straight as a die to the political action. It was all suddenly so clear. And so simple.

He had explained it to Melissa. And thinking of Melissa, he felt the warmth moving swiftly into his crotch. Ah, that girl was a delight! He only hoped that she had arrived safely at Cold Rock and would be there when he came in. What luck! Well, he mustn't think too much about that. Otherwise, he was laying himself open to possible disappointment. You could never count on the stage line. Not these days. Yet she should be there. She had the time to get there, even with delays. And in spite of himself he now found his thoughts riveted on the girl, on that luscious body with its tingling tits, its massive bush, and those unbelievable legs and buttocks.

The bouncing of the ambulance seemed to increase and only added to his sexual arousal, to the point where his erection was thrusting against his trouser leg and he thought that if this kept up he might even come.

Except that he didn't. It required massive self-control, and even the arousal of anger to avoid it. But Ralph Rumpel was a man of a very practical vision. And, horny as he was for the girl, and absolutely in the grip of the most extreme passion, the slave of his erection, he yet remembered that the ultimate was only improved by delay—if not too lengthy a delay —and so he held off, fighting himself under control. And by the time the ambulance reached their destination he was a whole lot calmer.

At the same time, he was most happy to discover that the sexual excitement had stimulated his creative faculties and so one or two knotty pieces in his plan suddenly unraveled and all was clear.

He related this to his companion—Melissa—as they lay supine on the clean flannel sheets that she always carried with her, at his request. Ralph was fastidious, and his lady friend appreciated that. Thus the sheets and other articles were always transported just in case primitive conditions were suddenly forced on one. Things like soap, colognes, liquid refreshments, cigars, bonbons, little biscuits for late or in-between snacks: all those necessary etceteras that helped make life possible, or at least bearable in the world of the frontier, commerce, the gaming hall, or—the best yet—the halls of government. For it was toward the government that Ralph Rumpel's star pointed. For a long time—for some years, in fact— his aim had been small: money, a game here and there, a theater in Virginia City, a bordello in San Francisco, the fanciest gambling establishment in

San Antonio, even a complete riverboat with its gambling and entertainment under his total command—all this paled in the light of his new dream. Politics. It was for this he'd been created. His name would go down in history.

And the prize was within reach. He'd come a long way, and while the fight was not yet over, he was on top of it. Each action, each detail, every single thing pointed to the final conclusion.

That very night, after reaching Cold Rock in the Army ambulance, he had told it again to Melissa as they both lay relaxed, satiated in the sanctity of complete sexual release.

"Just as I've tried to explain it to you, my dear, realize that before a territory is voted the status of a state, it has one congressional representative—a delegate. Under the rules of Congress, delegates cannot vote, however."

"But Bunny, what good does that do you? I mean, if you aren't allowed to vote, why be a delegate?" And she snuggled against his naked body, eager to hear more. And yet more.

Ralph Rumpel sighed. Sometimes the mere thought of what was so close to his grasp sent a riot of thrills through his body. He could hardly believe it. He! Himself! "Little Carly" they'd called him in the orphanage back in Chicago. And now. Now look at him. It was almost more than a man could handle. An orphan, the streets of the cities, the saloons and whorehouses and gambling dens, the slickers and the whoremongers and pimps, the killers and pugs. And he'd been through it all. He! Little Carly!

He had held thousands of dollars in his hands. And

soon, power. A delegate. The delegate. It was true what Melissa said, what was the point of being a delegate if a delegate had no vote? But the point was, the delegate had a power other men in government did not. A delegate wielded power. And that was the point. The club that the delegated wielded was a powerful one in the corridors of the nation's capitol. The country's ten territorial delegates worked in fairly close accord, for their problems were often similar; and because the territories covered about half the geographical area of the entire nation, the power had real clout. A delegate such as Ralph Rumpel hoped, planned, and intended to become had no vote, but he did have very much the ear of the Congress.

Yes, there would be power in his hands. And money. Lots of it.

And now, as Melissa snuggled closer to him, he found that he was holding something other than money or power in his hand. Well, a different sort of power. And he leaned over to kiss it.

And then all at once, without any warning, and without any possibility of explanation, he felt, as he kissed her breast, that his eyes were burning.

7

Almost any afternoon you could find the old man sitting outside Pop Tilghman's Livery, sitting in the sunlight, sometimes whittling, sometimes talking to anyone who might happen by, and then often just sitting as the afternoon turned into evening while the sun slowly went down behind the big mountains.

He was an old man, but he wasn't infirm. He wasn't much for talking, but he knew how to listen. He'd talk to the kids who'd sometimes come by and ask him questions about the country when the Indians and Trappers were more about, or how he found the gold. That was the big thing, the big excitement. How Henry "Old Hank" Larrabee found the gold.

But then much of the time Old Hank sat alone. Sometimes one or more of the town dogs would come by to sniff him, and he'd pet them some if he was of a mind to right then, or he might talk to them. The reporter from the paper that had started up in town, the *Cold Rock Crier*, came by and listened to Old Hank tell it. But then when the story came out in print it was somehow different. Hank didn't complain. He didn't read the story himself, not knowing how to read, but some young fellow had obliged and read it to him. And it wasn't much like he'd told it.

Old Hank didn't mind. He knew the story. He *was* the story. Who could know it any better than himself, then? And he liked to sit outside Pop Tilghman's Livery in the late afternoon and evening and listen to himself telling himself how it was. How it really was. . . .

It had been late in the afternoon when Hank and the party accompanying him had given up on trying to prospect by the stream in the shadow of Rattle Mountain. They were running out of supplies, and the Indians were not friendly, and there was nothing to do but admit defeat and slink back to Bannack, where they'd started from. Tired, really discouraged, they had just started back and were only about sixty miles out of Bannack, when suddenly—Hank never knew why but the notion just hit him like that—suddenly he called a halt and had suggested pitching camp. The others were for pushing on.

"Look around," Hank had said. "We'll never find a spot like this again. This ain't just a campin' spot. It—it's like a garden."

Hank Larrabee for sure was a rough, hardened miner and a hellraising frontiersman to boot; but he was also an artist. He stopped the party in a narrow valley rich in soft spring greens and dotted with a fabulous array of bright wildflowers. A dancing stream, pure and cool, raced swiftly through the valley. On each side, like they were watching, stood a line of shady alders and alder brush, graceful and pure in their simple presence. And even as he pointed the scene out to his companions, a young antelope drank without fear at the bank of the purling water.

There was no arguing with Hank when he spoke with that kind of authority, which he seemed to have naturally. And so the group camped, and after a short while their hopes seemed to revive. After a meal of elk, two of the party tended the mounts while the others took picks and shovels to a nearby ravine.

Hank was tethering a pony when all at once he straightened up as though some silent call had reached him. He let his eyes search the landscape— not as an artist now, but rather as a miner.

Suddenly he called out to one of the party. "Fletch! Get some tools. Hurry it! That rimrock there, I got to take a crack at it!"

Fletch brought pick and shovel, and Hank filled a pan with rock he chipped from an outcropping.

"Go wash that," he said. "Maybe we'll make some tobacco money, leastways."

Fletch had gone to the creek and had the fill half panned down when he spotted gold. And at that moment Hank's busy picking stopped at the edge of the slope. He called out, "Fletch, I got a scad here!"

Fletch stared at the residue in his pan, not believing what his eyes were seeing. "You got *a* scad, Hank? By God, man, I've got a *hundred*!"

Well, as Old Hank told it, maybe for the thousandth time, Fletch had "come down and I panned what he had and I seen he had a good prospect. It weighed at $2.40. And another the same. Not bad. Four dollars and eighty cents, by God!"

That was how he told it—to himself, and to anyone else who'd listen. Not so many now. Hardly any, actually, for the boom had hit. And everybody was off digging like their life depended on it.

Anyways, that first night up on Rattle Mountain they'd celebrated, and the next day they split into pairs and panned all day. All they'd actually wanted was a grubstake, figuring they'd come back later for the hard dig when they were better equipped.

Two days later they staked the ground in one-hundred-foot claims both for themselves and for their old friends, in line with the code of loyalty among miners.

Then the six decided on a solemn vow. Nobody in Bannack was to learn of the strike except trusted friends. Oaths were sworn. Hands were clasped.

But within days the secret was out and the valley overrun. The town appeared. Cold Rock. Even Hank didn't know how it got that name. But it stuck. And it boomed. For a short while the old man had liked it. The good times. Everybody was making it rich.

But then Torb Wellers had ridden into town. In a trice, or so it seemed to the more sober citizens, Torb Wellers was elected sheriff of nearby Bannack and a huge surrounding territory.

Outwardly Wellers was respectable as a deacon, and was greatly admired by Bannack's best people. No one realized that his periodic absences from Bannack were spent with his gang of road agents, gunslingers, bank robbers, and murderers, who recognized him as their secret boss. In only a short while no one was safe in Bannack, in Cold Rock, or anywhere within miles of the Torb Wellers gang.

Actually, it was Clarence Roller who told that part of the story to John Slocum. Slocum had of course heard a lot about Wellers. And as they rode north with Rumpel's three thousand head of Texas longhorns, Roller filled him in on details, including what had happened to Old Hank Larrabee, the discoverer of all that gold that had spawned such a wave of crime.

"Hank, he up and took off. He couldn't stand seeing what happened. First, all the gold crazies coming in and wrecking everything in the valley there, see— all mud, and all the jerry-built buildings, and the stink and noise. It got to him. See, Hank was a wilderness man. Sure, he wanted gold, but only enough for a stake. Hank knew the next horizon always had a valley more beautiful than today's. But he couldn't stand what happened to his friends—and to strangers, too."

"He felt responsible for them," Slocum put in, nodding his head a little as he saw the picture that Roller was drawing. He already knew about the Wellers gang—how hardly a night or day passed without somebody getting killed or robbed.

"The old boy's come back to town, I've heard," Roller told him. "And I hear he looks like an old man. Hell, he ain't my age hardly. But they say he looks ninety-some."

"So what's all this to do with you and me and Rumpel?" Slocum asked finally.

They had both been riding point that day and had stopped to breathe their horses, and water them too in a creek that wound down from the mountains lying ahead of them. They were close to Cold Rock.

"You got me."

They were seated now, chewing on beef jerky,

smoking, and Slocum had heated up some old Arbuckle coffee. He produced a couple of sourdough biscuits "to make the meal," as he put it to Roller.

"I heard the vigilantes took over," Slocum said. "I mean, about everybody knows that now. Wellers got himself a vigilante collar, and most of his gang, too."

"That's what I know too," Roller said. He had taken out his tobacco papers and sack of tobacco and was building a smoke, his thick, hairy fingers moving easily at the task, Slocum noticed. He knew the man had to be fast with that Smith & Wesson. But he still couldn't figure out what he and Roller were doing together. Suddenly he made a stab in the dark.

"I heard it was Boyd Flanagan heading the vigilantes that wiped out the Wellers gang," he said. And he watched the other man's face to see his reaction.

For just a split second there was something. He was sure of it. But what? It was a reaction, for sure. But how to read it? Was it surprise at the thought of Boyd Flanagan being the head of the vigilantes in Cold Rock? But was that only after Wellers and his gang had been strung up? But then why had Rumpel mentioned Flanagan in relation to the Fort Worth vigilantes?

"What makes you say that?" Roller asked, squinting at him through a little cloud of cigarette smoke pluming up under his wide hat brim.

"You tell me," Slocum said. He adjusted himself now as he sat facing the other man. He had been sitting cross-legged, and now he moved to a squatting position, still holding his mug of coffee, but now with his forearms on his thighs and his mug of coffee in his left hand. These points, he knew, were not lost on Clarence Roller, who remained as he was, sitting cross-legged, and drinking his coffee slowly.

"I knew it," Roller said. "Figured you likely knew it too."

"And if my thinking is correct—and it usually is—then I'm saying Boyd Flanagan and his vigilantes have taken over from the Wellers gang."

"Looks like it, don't it," Roller said.

"And Flanagan is working with Rumpel. I say ten will get you twenty on that one."

Roller was squinting at him from beneath his hat brim. "You know where the cattle fit in?" he said. "Or you an' myself?"

"Rumpel claims to be wanting to start Cold Rock as a shipping point," Slocum said.

"That's what he told me."

"Do you believe that?"

Without any hesitation, Roller shook his head.

"Then why is he sending this herd north? He'll make money, that's sure, but not all that much. And the gold's going to give out in Cold Rock, if it hasn't already. I made some inquiries before I left Fort Worth."

"You know the name Dunroodie?" Roller asked suddenly.

"Never heard it."

"Cotton Dunroodie."

"What about him?"

"He's the man I been looking for. I tracked him to Rumpel. Rumpel don't know that. Leastways, I don't believe he knows it."

Slocum canted his head at the other man. "I think he does. I have got a notion he does know it."

He watched the surprise hit. "How you figure?"

"How come he hired you?"

Roller's lips pursed at that, as he studied what those words could mean.

"Rumpel is smart as a whip," Slocum went on. "He's got a brain like a razor. That man doesn't make a move without it has a damn good reason and for his own benefit. So why did he hire you?"

"Told me to keep an eye on you. Put it like I could help you, was how he said. Course I knew what he meant. Keep an eye on you, and report to him."

"And if I stepped out of line, then kill me."

"He didn't say that," Roller came back sharply.

"He didn't have to, did he?"

Roller said nothing to that.

Slocum stood up. "Excepting, I don't take you for a hired killer, Roller. You sure you never been a lawman?"

A grin came into Roller's face then. "It 'pears to me it's you who need to be sure about that, Slocum."

They stood facing each other, both with their thumbs hooked in their belts.

"We'll be at Cold Rock tomorrow forenoon," Slocum said. He started to move toward his pony, who was ground-hitched nearby. Then he stopped and turned back to face Roller. "No," he said. "It ain't me who needs to be sure you're not a lawman, or might've been one. I think it's you, my friend. And don't make the mistake of underestimating Rumpel."

Roller said nothing to that, and Slocum checked his pony's head stall, then his cinch, and then he mounted, and without another look at Roller, he lifted the spotted horse to a brisk canter as he pointed him toward the herd.

He was looking forward to tomorrow. He was looking forward to seeing how right his new hunches were that had just come to him during the past day or two. He was looking forward to Montana.

They had been lucky so far, Slocum told himself. More then lucky. There had been no confrontation with Falling Lance and his Sioux. Nor with any rustlers. But he didn't let his guard down. That last night before reaching Cold Rock, he made the rounds of his sentries carefully, making sure that no one was taking anything for granted just because they were within reach of their destination.

Of course, any attack by the Indians now would be out of their assigned territory, and as such would be declared as "open hostility." Of course, Slocum realized, any fighting the Sioux might engage in within their assigned territory would also be considered hostile to the peace.

Slocum was a little surprised that they hadn't had more trouble with the warriors, especially if there had been whiskey going into the tribes. He knew that the chiefs couldn't always control their warriors, even without the problem of whiskey. The young men were restless, and resentful too of the white invaders. All the same, he had heard of various attacks among the settlers along the way up from Texas. And of course, there was the situation at Fort Tyson, where Falling Lance and his men had the Army pinned in their fort, which was looking more and more like a prison.

No, there was something wrong with the picture.
Slocum knew it in his bones, his skin, his blood.
That they had gotten this far without a major encounter with the Indians was not just a miracle—
there was something damned suspicious about it. As
a consequence, he doubled the guards that night, and
he himself slept lightly, fully clothed, and with his
weapons right at hand.

And suddenly he was wide awake. The footstep
was unmistakable. But he knew it had to be one of
the men on guard duty. It was Turk, whom he'd first
encountered in the Chip House in Fort Worth.

"There's a caravan off to the southeast." Turk's
words came swift with urgency.

Slocum was already on his feet as the man appeared out of the shrubbery. "That bunch that were at
Antelope?"

"Dunno. There's about four wagons."

"What d'you mean *about* four wagons," Slocum
snapped, keeping his voice down, however.

"Harris said four, but somebody else said five.
That's what Jerry Thimes got from Goose."

"What a bunch of knotheads!" Slocum growled at
him.

"You want me with you?" Turk asked, impervious
to Slocum's irritation.

"Get back to the herd. I'll be checking out those
caravans. Damn it, them coming in this close."

"You figurin' they might attract some of them
Sioux, do you?"

"I do. But there isn't much we can do about it.
We'll double the guard anyway. Now get going."

It didn't take him long to get the men necessary

for reinforcing the sentries. Most of them were awake anyway. After giving his orders he made his way quickly to where the wagons were camped. The first person he ran into was a sentry, a boy of about eighteen. "Who's in charge?" he asked.

"Dutch Wagner," the boy said. He was chewing tobacco and spitting. "Where you from, mister? I seen you at Antelope, I do believe."

"I'm with that herd of cattle," Slocum said.

"Is there Injuns about?" the boy asked nervously.

"There is, and I want you to douse that fire, I mean pronto. What the hell's the matter with you, lighting a fire so's the whole Sioux Nation knows where you are!"

At that point a beefy man appeared. "You're John Slocum!"

"You better get that fire out, mister. I mean fast. Though by now the Sioux have got to know you're here. And that means they know where we are."

The beefy man looked only slightly chastened. "I'm Dutch Wagner. I figured we was out of hostile country by now, Slocum."

"Mister, in this territory a man is never out of hostile country. It's a good notion to remember that if you want to keep your scalp."

"I've heard that the Injuns don't attack at night."

"Look, get that fire out, double your guards, and I want to talk to your men. I mean right now."

"Pushy, ain't you, mister." The man said it calmly, not like anyone eager to fight for his stance, but as though he was remarking on the weather.

"Mister, when you come in here like this, letting the whole country know you're here, and you camp right next to my herd, you are then including me in your stupidity. I don't much like that. Do you understand me? I don't want my cattle and men slaughtered on account of your dumbness. Now get your men here. Fast!"

It shook the beefy man then. And within minutes he had the men and some of the women too collected where Slocum could talk to them.

He was fast, and he was to the point. "Check your weapons. Get your wagons in a circle, and unhitch your animals. Keep your saddle horses spread out, not all bunched where the Sioux can stampede 'em. But keep them saddled. Stay with your group. You make three groups, each wagon is a group. And each group has a leader. Check your weapons, your ammo; then take your positions. You men on guard, you pull a two-hour shift. Make that one hour. I don't want anyone falling asleep." He paused, searching through the dim light but not recognizing any of them really. "You work out the shifts. And remember—the time you have to be especially careful and alert is just when you're changing guard with somebody. Whoever's out there will be watching for that moment when your attention is caught and you're not watching, not listening."

Suddenly a woman's voice said, "I'm scared, mister."

Slocum looked toward the dark area where the voice had come from. "Miss," he said, "or Missus, I'm scared too."

When they had dispersed, Wagner approached and said, "But Slocum, ain't it true that the Injuns don't fight at night? I'm serious. I heard that."

"The Indians will fight you anytime, anyplace, all night long or all day, Mr. Wagner." He started to turn away. "You had better believe that," he added, turning back to face Wagner. "Whether you believe it or not, just believe it. Otherwise, you don't have a prayer of a chance."

And he left them and walked back to his herd. It was just then, as he heard one of the longhorns snort, that he realized he hadn't seen the girl, Norah.

Then suddenly he heard the crackle of underbrush behind him and he spun, his hand streaking to his six-gun.

"Slocum."

It was her. He could smell her. He could almost feel her.

"I just want to say thank you. Or maybe hello, or something."

And she was right in front of him.

"Are you all right?" he asked.

"I think so. Of course I'm scared, just as Sonya said. We're all scared. Even the men, I guess. Because all we've heard of since we left Antelope was all this stuff about Indians attacking."

"It doesn't seem to bother your man Dutch, your leader."

"I don't know. Dutch is pretty hard. I guess he's got more courage than some of us."

"Your courage seems to be doing pretty well, I'd say."

"I just wanted to say hello. I hope it's all right to have followed you like that."

"I'm glad you did. But I want to ask you, what about the other men? Are they like Dutch—I mean all cool and not afraid? Because none of you appear to be experienced as far as Indians and this kind of country go."

"I'd say the men are also having a hard time, but not as bad as the women."

"But Dutch seems all right. Doesn't show his feelings. That it?"

"That's what it seems like. Why do you ask? You seem to be especially interested in Dutch."

He shrugged. "Not especially, but since he's your leader, it's a good thing he doesn't get rattled. That's all. Wouldn't you agree with that?"

"Yes. Yes, I think it's good he keeps his head like that. Not that the others haven't kept their heads. No one has acted badly. Not any of the men, or the women either."

"You be careful," Slocum said then. And he reached out and touched her arm.

"I'm very glad to see you, Slocum."

"Interesting how you bump into friends now and again, isn't it?" he said.

She gave a little laugh. "You're very good to me," she said. And then she turned and was gone.

He found the camp quiet, when he returned. Yet there was also an air of expectancy. Good enough, he decided. It was the atmosphere he wanted. It wasn't good to have anyone complacent, the way he'd felt the wagon train had been—probably due to Dutch Wagner's attitude. And he found himself wondering whether the man was naturally phlegmatic like that. On the other hand, he was beginning to toy with a strange notion that had invaded his mind. He wasn't sure of it, really, it hadn't yet come to any point where he could have formulated it. It was vague, more a feeling, really, than a thought.

When he reached his bedding he found that he wasn't ready for sleep. And so he sat nearby, with his back against a cottonwood tree, wide awake, letting his thoughts on his situation take him wherever they wished.

But still nothing definite came. After a while he lay down on his bedding and slept.

He had been expecting the Sioux to hit them ever since they'd left Laramie. In fact, it was what more than one of the various Army officers had predicted. But outside of a few skirmishes, and the one fight before reaching Tyson, there had been nothing of any consequence. Slocum had tended to put this down to the fact that Falling Lance must be needing all his warriors for keeping Gallup and his men pinned down. Yet he wasn't really satisfied with that explanation. On the other hand, it could be that the word had gotten to the tribes that the cowboys were well equipped with the new Remingtons, whose firepower and speed of reloading were far and away beyond anything the Sioux could get up. Yes, it had to be that.

These were the thoughts with which he had just awakened, and then he smelled something in the air and felt the electricity. But the storm was ahead of him as he all but jumped to his feet. It hit like a hundred hammers, the thunder rolling through the charging sky, as lightning flashed in great forks from horizon to horizon, illuminating the suddenly frantic herd of longhorns, soaking them as they stirred and rambled over the shining ground, while the rain pelted down on everything.

A sudden blinding flash of lightning followed instantly by a sharp crack of thunder illumined the stricken animals. The churning sky, ripping and crackling, released buckets of rain, drenching men and animals indiscriminately. The cuffs of Slocum's jacket were instantly soaking at his wrists, but he was too busy barking orders to his men to notice.

"Hold them against the creek!" he ordered, shouting in between the claps of thunder.

A sudden crash of thunder hit like a blow, seeming as though it would tear the sky apart. Slocum, looking up suddenly, caught the flashes of blue lightning sizzling through the black, soaking night, while the thunder boomed with the ferocity of artillery. It flashed suddenly through his head that it was a dance, as that great wall of thunder and boiling sky suddenly closed in on them, and then as suddenly would retreat in a blazing light to regroup into a new pattern and again attack.

It lasted maybe twenty minutes and then stopped with the same suddenness as it had begun, leaving in its aftermath an astonishment at the extent of its ferocity while in action, and the quality of its calm after it was done. Such storms always struck Slocum in this manner. And he felt as though something large, heavy, and thick had been removed. At the same time, he was grateful that the men had been able to hold the herd. Another five minutes and they would have stampeded.

Now the sky began to regain its clarity. The air was still wet with the storm that had gone away, but the sky was clearing, and Slocum saw toward the east that it would shortly be dawn.

"Reckon if there was them damn Injuns out there, the bastards'd be too soakin' wet to give us any trouble." The voice, coming from nowhere, crackled with humor and goodwill into the now starry night. And Slocum saw that the sky was lightening, the dawn was coming quickly. And he had that warning sense of something that he had known almost all his life.

The sun rose brilliant into the wet air, a tremendous burning orb, riveting in its demand for attention. And John Slocum reached for his Remington, and fast. For they were there, without the slightest warning other than the feeling Slocum had in his guts. A wave of screaming Indians riding up and out of a hidden draw with the sun at their backs burning into the eyes of the startled cattlemen. It was as though they had erupted right out of the ground.

Two men were hit, while Slocum accounted for one brave with a bullet through his neck. The Indians suddenly disappeared, having ridden right through the disordered, rain-drenched camp, screeching at the cattle, firing arrows and old flintlocks at the cowboys, the cattle, the picketed horses.

They were gone, leaving one cowboy with an arrow in his shoulder and two others with slight wounds. But they had not gone unscathed. A warrior lay dead, and two others were clearly wounded. Slocum saw them riding off with two other warriors, supporting them on their horses.

Almost instantly there was the sound of Winchesters and handguns firing on the other side of a big stand of cottonwoods. Then—silence.

The men had gathered around Slocum, wondering what had happened.

"Sounds like those Indians might've run into some kind of ambush," Slocum said to Dutch Wagner as the beefy man came striding toward him.

"How do you figure?"

"Those were Winchesters and handguns, of which the Sioux didn't have a one. So it has to be whites."

"Likely the Army," the beefy man said. "Let's hope so."

"It isn't the Army," Slocum said. He lifted his voice then. "You men get on the herd. We'll be moving out now. Keep 'em bunched but not too tight, and move 'em slow. I don't want them all hassled. Another set like that and we'll likely lose the lot."

But Dutch Wagner wasn't satisfied. "Ain't you gonna take a look, find out what all that shootin' was about?" he asked Slocum's back as he mounted his spotted pony.

Looking down at the man who was standing there with one hand in his hip pocket, the other hanging down at his side, Slocum said quietly, "That ain't our business any longer, Mr. Wagner. But we'll more than likely be hearing about it directly. That's how I see it."

And as he spoke they heard the horses, and in the next moment the riders appeared, coming through the trees into the large clearing where the men were starting the cattle.

8

He was a big man, and his big red face seemed to be all mouth and eyes. Even though seated on that big steel-dust gelding he was tall. The three guns he was packing in his holsters and cartridge belt were not there for decoration.

But John Slocum didn't even look at the big man and his dozen riders as they came swiftly through the trees and into the clearing where he was giving orders to his men and seeing that the two who had been hit were taken care of.

"Who's ramrodding this here outfit?" the big man called out, and he suddenly drew the pistol from his belt.

"Don't fire that!"

And it was John Slocum standing right there in front of that big man and his big horse.

"Figure it'll spook the beef, do you?" The rider's red face split into a huge grin. Wagging his head, he slid the pistol back into his belt. "You be Slocum, huh?"

Slocum still said nothing. He just stood there, watching the man on the horse and his companions.

"That's Slocum for sure," one of the riders said.

"That's what I know," said the man with the red face. "For sure it ain't me who is the famous John Slocum. Me, I'm just poor little old Boyd Flanagan. Boo-hoo!"

An appreciative titter of laughter ran through the group of riders then. And suddenly Boyd Flanagan was serious. "Ain't you gonna thank the Cold Rock Vigilance Committee for shooing them nasty Injuns away from your precious beef, Mr. Slocum?" And he leaned forward now, his forearms on the pommel of his big stock saddle, his eyes laughing. Then, not waiting for an answer, his eyes swept the cowboys and the men and women from the wagon train.

"I got two things to say," Slocum was standing easy, with his thumbs hooked in his gunbelt. "And I'll say them once. Number one, those Indians were sent packing by these men and women here, Flanagan, and you better remember that. And to you men . . ." His gaze swept the cowboys near him. "Get that herd moving before these damn fools do something else plumb stupid!"

There was a split second of charged silence, and then Slocum said, "Move!"

Boyd Flanagan was grinning. "I could sure use a feller like you, Slocum, with us vigilantes. I like your guts."

But Slocum had turned toward his spotted pony and now stepped into the stirrup and mounted. Without a look in the direction of Flanagan and his riders he kicked his pony into a fast walk. Looking down at Dutch Wagner, he said, "You'd best follow us in, Wagner. But you do what you like."

As he rode toward the creek, then, he thought he

saw Norah, at the back of the group, but he didn't let that distract him. He had scored on Flanagan, and it felt good. At the same time he knew he was really going to have to watch his backtrail now.

Slocum hadn't been in town twenty minutes before he heard it. How the Cold Rock vigilantes had saved Hector Kinsolving's herd of Texas longhorns and thirty drovers plus the men and women of a wagon train from the depredations of the bloodthirsty Sioux.

It was in the saloon, in the rooming house where he signed the register, in the Rocky Eatery where he filled up on some down-home cooking, and it seemed even in the air.

Hector Kinsolving had an office on the main street of the town, and it was here that Slocum appeared with the envelope Rumpel had given him to be handed over on delivery.

"We can all be thankful that the vigilantes were on hand, eh, Slocum?" And the short man with the potbelly, spectacles, and red galluses puckered his mouth in emphasis of the importance he evidently felt for those words.

"Might have been better if they'd showed up on time," Slocum observed smoothly.

Kinsolving's eyebrows lifted, his face reddened slightly, and he reached for his cigar, which he had placed on the edge of his desk. "What do you mean by that?"

"I'm only saying what everybody who was there knows—that we'd already driven 'em off."

"Well, well—well I don't know about that."

"You know about it now, mister, on account of I am telling you. Your vigilante boys and what's-his-name started shooting at the Sioux when they took off after running into us. That's the straight of it. And I am not listening to any bullshit put out by that asshole who was ramrodding 'em." Slocum said his words hard, but not with heat. His anger was of the cold variety.

"You're saying that Boyd Flanagan wasn't giving us the straight of it." Kinsolving leaned onto his desk, the fingers of his right hand drumming nervously onto some loose papers. "I should tell you that I am a lawyer, Slocum, and what you're suggesting is that Flanagan was not telling the truth. I find that passing strange. Why, Boyd Flanagan—"

But Slocum had listened to enough. "Look, Kinsolving, you've got your herd. They're in good shape. The delivery is made. Now you can pay me and the boys."

"Of course, of course, Slocum." He leaned back, drummed his fingers on the edge of the desk, then opened the drawer. His belly, which was not small, got in the way, and he had to move his chair back. "Here. You can count it. I know you'll find it intact." And he handed the thick envelope to Slocum, who was still standing.

Taking the envelope, Slocum hefted it in his hand. Then he pulled a chair closer to where he was standing and sat down, pushing his hat onto the back of his head.

"I assure you, it's all there," Kinsolving said, and began again to drum his fingers on the desktop.

"And I assure you I am going to count it to assure myself," Slocum said.

And he took his time. He was tempted at one point to stop and start over as though he'd made a mistake, but he didn't. When he was through he stood up. "Good enough. I reckon you'll be writing or maybe seeing Rumpel," Slocum said.

"I expect to see him, Slocum. Mr. Rumpel is here. He is in Cold Rock."

Slocum lifted his eyebrows in mock surprise. "By jingo, that man sure likes to get around, don't he?" And he grinned.

"He is here, of course, for the big campaign," Kinsolving said. "You must be aware of that," he said, smiling. "The campaign. Nobody could be in town five minutes without becoming aware of the important event in our lives here in Cold Rock. But I won't bore you with the details." He stood up suddenly, a whole foot shorter than Slocum. "Congratulations, sir, on your cattle drive. I realize the difficulties. I know that you have performed heroic work." He came around the desk then and stood in front of Slocum. "I feel certain that Mr. Rumpel will offer you other work."

"I am pretty certain about that too," Slocum said with a slow smile, mostly at the corners of his mouth. He started toward the door of Kinsolving's office then, but stopped and, turning back, said, "'Bout how far is it to the reservation?"

"You planning on visiting the Blackfeet? I'd say it's pretty close. Too close for most people to feel comfortable. Why?"

"You said Blackfeet."

"That is what I've heard. I have not visited the reservation. I've not had occasion to."

"But they were Sioux hit us down by the creek," Slocum said. "And they were a long ways off from Falling Lance's tribe and the rest of the Sioux."

"I don't understand what you're saying," Kinsolving said, his tone guarded suddenly. "An Indian's an Indian. And he'll as soon kill you and scalp you as take a drink."

"Alcohol you mean?"

"I do not mean spring water."

Slocum had his hand on the doorknob when Kinsolving spoke again. "I'd be very careful, Slocum, about riding out to wherever the Indians are located. I have heard wild stories. Wild."

"Then how do you know they're true?"

"They're true. No question. They've got to be true, Slocum."

Slocum said, "Where's Rumpel?"

"You could try the Nugget House."

Kinsolving was still standing at the side of his desk, his extended fingertips touching some papers at his side, as his visitor left.

"You heard?"

"Every word." Ralph Rumpel coughed gently into his fist as he closed the door of the room adjoining Hector Kinsolving's office and then walked over and sat down in an easy chair by the window.

Kinsolving brought up a straightback chair and seated himself at a reasonable distance from the man in the easy chair. "Well, what do you think?"

Rumpel made a face to match the shrug he gave

with his shoulders. "You see what he is. He is no one to get fancy with."

"I can sure figure that out," Kinsolving said ruefully. "And apparently he wasn't taking anything from Flanagan."

"Flanagan is suitably burned," Rumpel said, reaching to an inner pocket of his coat for a cigar.

"But Boyd Flanagan is not a man to be put down. I'm sure you'll agree, Ralph."

"That's why it's good to always have people around to play against each other," Rumpel observed in a sage tone.

His companion nodded. It was rough working with Ralph Rumpel, he told himself for maybe the hundredth time. You had to keep sharp as a tack. Otherwise . . . He had observed Ralph closely. Ralph offered no mercy. Ralph was only concerned with success. If his own mother . . . Well, he knew the rest of that one.

Ralph had been engaged wholly with his cigar—sniffing it, feeling its dryness, studying its shape. It was not stubby, not long and thin, but nicely in-between. He bit the little bullet of tobacco out of the rounded end and twirled the end in his lips until it was wet. He held the barrel of the Havana—and it was pure Havana tobacco—under his nose. Ah! Nothing like a good cigar.

He decided to say so. "There is nothing like a good cigar, Hector. I'm sure you will agree." And feeling expansive, he reached into his pocket again and handed one to his companion.

"Thank you, Ralph. Closest thing to a good woman, I'd venture to say."

Rumpel released a jolly chuckle at that. "You know the saying, and it is always worth repeating: A good woman's only a good woman, but a good cigar is a smoke."

And they both chuckled at that.

Turning to Kinsolving as he lighted his cigar and the room began to receive a cloud of smoke, he maised one eyebrow just slightly and his host got the message.

"I believe you'll find this an excellent brandy, Ralph," Hector said, reaching into the cupboard at the side of his desk.

"Same source?"

"Same source." Kinsolving chuckled and poured.

Rumpel cocked an eyebrow, his eyes glowing with anticipation as he inhaled the strong vapor. "There is no question about what's wrong with this world, Hector. It's as plain as the ace of spades."

Kinsolving lifted his glass and held it, not drinking, while he smiled, waiting to hear what Rumpel was going to deliver, ready to give suitable applause.

But Ralph didn't speak. He was tasting the brandy, even to the point of being so indelicate as to smack his lips, but refraining.

"And what is it, Ralph?" asked Hector, pleased at knowing the precise timing for his line.

"It's simple. The damn fools don't understand that the only answer to life is to live it—and goddamn well!"

And they both chortled over that one.

An hour later, as he lay delightfully exhausted beside Melissa, his eyes played lightly around a water stain on the ceiling above their bed, and he said, "You know, my dear, there's no question about what's wrong with this world. It's as plain as the ace of spades."

"But Bunny, I think it's a wonderful world. I don't see a thing wrong with it!" And she sat up suddenly, turning toward him as her right breast bounced against his face.

The next thing he knew he was sucking on her wholly erect nipple with a fervor that caused her to squeal with delight.

And then he was mounting her, driving his rigid organ high and deep, grinding its head up into her as far as it could go, while she squirmed and thrust her buttocks and gasped at the vigor of his member. "It's so big, Bunny. Oh, I love it so! More! More! More!"

Until in a rush of blind, exquisite consummation they rode each other until they collapsed into total bliss, lying still in their embrace, exhausted, totally satiated.

"You horny old man," she whispered happily in his ear.

"You hot little creature!"

"You rutting bull!"

"You delicious seductress!"

"I want more."

"Now?"

"Whenever you're ready. Darling, I crave you. I need you, don't you understand that. I need you to service me."

"Continually?" he asked, feeling his penis stirring.

"Endlessly. Copiously. Forever-ously!!"

And they giggled at that as she lowered herself to take him in her mouth.

When he had flooded her again, he asked, almost gasping it, "Are you satisfied now, you gorgeous devil?"

"Oh yes, I'm always satisfied by you, Bunny." And she snuggled close to him. "You know what I mean? I mean—like for a while, you know?"

"How long a while?" he asked, scratching at an itch on his right buttock.

"Well . . . How long? Well, maybe like . . ." And as she spoke she reached over and began playing with his balls. "Like—now, Bunny?"

This time they fell asleep afterwards. They must have slept for a long time, for when he awakened he saw that night had fallen. It was dark out in the street.

Beside him Melissa was breathing evenly, sound asleep. He looked down at her, though he couldn't see her in the dark. He sat up, bringing his feet down to the floor. Quietly, being careful not to disturb her, he lighted the coal-oil lamp on the bureau, then turned the flame down low so it wouldn't awaken her.

He stood by the side of the bed, looking at her, the curve of her high cheekbone as she lay on her side with one arm on the pillow above her head, the other lost inside the sheets, her brown hair spilling all over her arm and the pillow.

By God, he was thinking, she is beautiful. And he was a lucky man. Not that he didn't deserve her. He certainly did deserve such a lovely creature. But he valued her; at least he told himself that he valued her.

She was beautiful, she was bright, too, and she valued him. That was the big thing—that she looked up to him. Well, why shouldn't she?

He, by golly, looked up to himself. So many people did. And he had earned it. He had earned it through hard work, patience, brilliant strategies and campaigns, each of which increased his scope, led him higher toward his goal. The goal which he had only lately begun to really focus on. Government. Politics. Power.

All the rest of it—the gambling, the traveling, the barking and shilling, the cards and dice and horses and prizefighters and cockfighting and bearbaiting— all the whole kit-and-caboodle had led to this one thing, this one place, the top of the heap. Government. Washington!

Of course, the real climb was only beginning. This job, this job here in Cold Rock, in the territory, would be the first step in the new phase he was going into. All the rest had been preparation. For this. For this final climb to—well, who knew where!

He thought he would get some water. He was thirsty, and as a matter of fact, hungry. He wondered if he might slip out for something—some food, a drink.

All at once the bedcovers stirred and he felt a hand on his thigh. His penis registered it instantly.

"Bunny, can't you sleep?"

"I did sleep, my dear. But I'm wide awake now."

"You are?" And suddenly, like a jack-in-the-box, she sat straight up, her firm, curving breasts bouncing into the room, to his delight and instant erection.

"What's that moving those covers, Bunny? Have

you got something there under those sheets?"

"Why, it's nothing, my dear. Nothing."

"Bunny, don't tell me fibs. You've got something under there, and I want to see what it is." And her hand thrust inside the bedclothes and felt along his throbbing leg.

"It's . . ." he started to say, but she had his member now in her fist, and anything he might have said died on his dry lips.

"Bunny!" Her voice rose in delight as she gripped his absolutely rigid organ. And in the next moment she was down and under the covers, and he lay back, his legs falling apart.

"My God . . . My God, what are you doing? Darling! Melissa! Baby, what are you doing?"

But all Melissa could do was mumble.

Yet after a few moments, when he asked her again, barely able to speak he was so deep into total ecstasy, she did stop. But only for a couple of seconds. Only long enough to say, "Don't you know it's rude, Bunny, to talk with your mouth full?"

Out back of Pop Tilghman's Livery the afternoon was drowsy. "Like the backside of Cold Rock," Old Hank Larrabee had sometimes put it. "None of all that fuss-'n'-feathers shit goin' on. Though I am a one who also likes that stuff too. I mean, like the excitement. Exceptin' it ain't like it was. It ain't like it used to be." And his milky gray eyes would swim to the distant mountains.

John Slocum had been quick to take full note of Old Hank's appearance, sizing him up right off. He was glad to see the old man again, whittling a branch of cottonwood with his bowie knife. He looked like the poorest desert rat or mountain bum who had ever crawled in out of the open spaces. His clothes were close to rags, one foot showed through its shoe, and the other wasn't much better. He was patched with flour sacks and deerskin, and his beard and mustache and the hair on his head were snarled like a nest of rattlesnakes. He looked, Slocum decided, like the sole remaining member of some party that had died of thirst and starvation in the desert.

Slocum had brought in his spotted pony, given him a rubdown inside the livery, fed him oats, forked him some hay, and then wandered out the back door, which gave onto a soft evening vista.

"Heard you run into some of the natives," Hank said without even looking up at Slocum as he appeared in the big doorway of the barn.

"Had a little excitement there for a spell," Slocum allowed, speaking easy as he stepped out of the barn doorway and stood swing-hipped, with his hands pushed slightly inside his belt, his eyes on the horizon and the westering sun.

Some sound, something like a cackle, came from the bearded face beneath the chewed-up Stetson hat. Hank had still not looked at him. "Them vigilante boys run 'em off, did they?"

"They run 'em off after they'd already been run off," Slocum said quietly. Ordinarily he wouldn't have answered such a remark, but he liked the old man, and he respected him. Any man who wanted to sit all day like that in the weather, and could do it, had to have Slocum's respect.

Another cackle fell from beneath the wide, battered hat brim. "Figures. Flanagan and Hooligan and them boys." His shoulders began to shake, and Slocum realized the old man was laughing.

"Flanagan, he knows what he is doin', not that I personally favor what he does. But that Hooligan, shit, he can't find his own ass in the broad daytime. You mind me on that, mister."

Slocum gave a laugh. "I do believe it," he said. "But what's goin' on here with all this vigilante stuff, can you tell me? They had 'em running all over the place down in Fort Worth when I left there. Everybody's a vigilante now."

And all at once as he said those words, he made the connection with Rumpel. Coincidence, was it? Just that? Or was there something deeper here.

"They come in mostly *after* Torb Wellers was strung up. But they been tellin' it all over how it was themselves what caught Wellers and Lowdy and Rimshaw and the rest of them buggers. An' it wasn't, by God. It wasn't!" Suddenly the old man reared back and drove his fist into his other palm.

"But I reckon everybody knows that, don't they?" Slocum said, his tone reasonable, wondering why Hank had gotten so excited.

"Nope! You dunno, young feller, how people is. They don't remember nothin' from one minute to the next. An' that is a fact. That Flanagan bunch, they come in here and spread all that malarkey aroundabout. And all the damn fools from here to breakfast just been lappin' it up."

He stopped suddenly, slipped his hands under his dirty and torn old galluses, and sat there wagging his head back and forth and clucking and cursing.

"That seems to be the way of it with people, don't it," Slocum said. "Interesting, though."

The old man was silent.

Slocum tried again. "You're saying that Flanagan and his boys just came in after the regular vigilantes —whoever they were—cleaned up the gang, and then they took credit for it?"

"That is just exact and precise what I am sayin' right down to the jot and tittle of it, young feller. Those jaspers come in and filed claim on that good work done by Bill Eagleton and Charley Stuart. Sons-ofbitches. Well, hell, it ain't no hair off my ass. I don't mind nothin' but my own business anyways."

"Must have been pretty bad around here in the old days," Slocum said, still trying to open it up. "I mean when the Wellers gang ran it all."

"Them days . . . Them days!"

Slocum watched the old Stetson hat wag from side to side.

"Know what the paper said about this place then?"

"Can't say as I do."

"Said like life an' property depends entirely on a man's accuracy—get that?—accuracy and speed with a six-gun." Shit, we had Torb Wellers runnin' the law, and the sonofabitch was head of the bandits. Nobody knowed it! They had men set up every-wheres, telling Wellers when there was going to be shipments of ore, tellin' about what rich traveler was going to be takin' the stage, or a pack train some-place, and all like that so's Torb and the boys'd be waitin' for the stage, or whoever it was travelin'. Shit, they robbed and killed a man for his watch!

Took his timepiece and cut his throat! Bet you never run into the likes of that, mister!"

Slocum had heard about Hank Larrabee and how he was always telling the tall old-time tales of the way it was, and like how it used to be, and a man better not listen too long or he'd start believing all that malarkey from the old buzzard, who as any damn fool could see was plumb out of his head and didn't know his ass from a pick and shovel.

But Slocum heard something more in the story. Something in him began to turn it all over as he heard Old Hank spieling it. "How did they finally get next to Torb Wellers?" he asked.

"Charley Stuart and Bill Eagleton, they was the ones got together and did some good figurin'. By that time, o' course, nobody dared go out of his shack at night. Nobody was safe, man or boy. Well, Charley and Bill, they got together and organized the Stranglers."

"I've heard of them."

"Sure you have. I see you is educated, mister. Now, you ast me a question, and do not interrupt me till I get finished telling you the straight of it. Now then, you got some tobaccy on you? I could use a fresh chew."

Slocum didn't chew tobacco, but he had remembered noticing Hank's chewing the last time he'd seen him and had wisely bought a packet.

Hank Larrabee accepted the entire packet without a blink, and swept on with his narrative. "Charley, he'd been an Injun fighter, a miner, trader, freighter, packer, merchant, an' God knows what all else, an' he knew how to handle himself, let me tell you. I recollect the time—"

"Tell about Wellers and the vigilantes," Slocum said, interrupting fast. "I mean, if you've a mind to. But you were saying about how Stuart and Eagleton got things organized into a vigilance committee."

"They picked a dozen top men. And Stuart, well, the both of them actually, they was set not to hurt anybody innocent. Like they was careful not to make a mistake. So they gived the men they caught a chance. Usually give them a warning. One chance. If they showed up again then they hanged 'em. They took the whole bunch of Wellers' gang. About twenty-five men. Right up to finally getting Wellers and his closest ones, like Huggins and Beech Saunders and One-Eye Boone. They got least twenty-five, thirty men. Hanged 'em from the nearest tree that was to hand."

"And finally they got Wellers," Slocum said, prompting as Hank paused for a fresh chew.

"Finally they got to Wellers. Funny, he was the last man anybody suspected. What the hell, he was the sheriff. Had a helluva big lot of territory to handle, and everybody liked him. Good-looking man, educated. Some said he went to college back east. Had a good-looking wife. Everybody liked Torb Wellers. People used to ask his advice on things. He knew what he was talking about. It seemed like, anyways."

"I have heard that," Slocum said.

"What?"

"That Wellers was an educated man."

"So it come as a real big surprise when they dis-

cover the man they been lookin' for all this time was
one and the same feller that was leading posses looking for the killers and robbers and all like that. An' it
was by God the sheriff hisself!" And Old Hank Larrabee raised up again and slammed his right fist into
the palm of his left hand, three, four times. And then
spat vigorously on the ground in front of him.

"Can you tie that!" He grinned, his breath rasping
and smelling of aged tobacco and whiskey, and he
wiped his mouth free of spittle with the back of his
bony wrist.

Then a silence fell with the suddenness of a light
going out.

For a full minute or two neither spoke. The old
man's breath was sawing from the exertion of his
storytelling, while Slocum's thoughts were racing.
There was something he was missing, he felt. What
was it? Some point, some place in the story where
he'd felt that twinge of recognition, but then it had
slipped away.

Hank was looking down at a little lizard walking
between his legs. Without looking up he said, "You
might think that was the end of it, mister."

"Wasn't it."

"Take a look about." And turning his head
slightly, Hank Larrabee placed his left thumb against
his left nostril and shot the contents of his right nostril in the direction of that little lizard. But he didn't
score. Then, still using the same hand, simply press-
ing his left forefinger against his right nostril, he
cleared his other passage. He missed again. But he
was an old-timer and so remained nonplussed. This
time he let fly with a streak of brown and yellow

juice between his lips, getting an amount on his already yellow-stained beard, and even some on his shirt, but scoring partially on the streaking rear end of the small lizard.

Meanwhile, the sun was closer to the horizon. Slocum wanted to stay and get the old man to talk some more; at the same time, he didn't want to overdo it. He was just thinking of going in to check his pony again and talk to Pop Tilghman, who hadn't been there when he'd ridden in, but Hank started to talk some more.

"All I can say is this bunch of vigilantes we got now, they've cleaned up a lot of stuff. The town is safer, I do believe. The women has got to be happier about that. But there's still stuff goin' on. Stage was robbed last week, on the Lander run."

"You've got to expect some times that aren't going to be so smooth," Slocum said, just to keep the talk rolling. "You admit it's better than it was."

"That I do." He sniffed, and scratched deep into one armpit, then the other. "Dunno if it's better to have the vigilantes or the road agents, by God!"

"Tell me how long it was between Wellers' gang getting wiped out and the new sheriff coming in." It was the question Slocum had been wanting to ask for some time, but the old boy hardly allowed room for a hiccup in his great monologue.

"I dunno how long. Some weeks. Why? Stranger, why you want to know that? We got a sheriff in Cold Rock, but he is planted."

Suddenly the old man was looking at him with suspicion, and maybe even a certain fear in his face. Slocum wasn't sure. He did feel and see the change though, right in front of his eyes. Hank was afraid. Maybe not severely afraid, but there was definitely fear in his voice and in his manner now.

"Like to buy you a drink," Slocum said after a moment.

"Want me to talk some more, huh."

"Only if you've a mind to. Otherwise, I'd buy you a drink anyway. Figure to need one myself."

The old fellow seemed to be giving the suggestion serious thought, and Slocum simply waited, saying nothing, but with his mind working on all that Hank Larrabee had just told him.

Presently, Hank let out a great sigh, stood up, scratched himself in each armpit again, then in his crotch, spat, sniffed, spat again, belched, and looked at his companion with a very pleasant smile on his face. "I been taking my time deciding which saloon to take our business to, or your business, actually, since it'll be yourself does the payin'."

And with a cackle he started out, walking with a slight limp, but not stove up by any means. There was a quiet vigor in him that Slocum easily caught, and which he also saw as unique. He liked Hank Larrabee.

9

One afternoon at Fancy Dan Diamond's Lost Mine Saloon, a group of earnest poker players sat hunched around a baize-topped table while a small group of hangers-on stood behind them, glued to each and every play.

It was jacks or better, and the game wasn't dragging at all. The betting was brisk, and the players were enjoying every minute of the action, as were the onlookers.

Three of the seven players were none other than the whiskey-train operators who had stripped the Indians at the same game out on the prairie only just recently. Besides Clancy O'Rourke, Ollie Wirehouse, and Three-Fingers Barney Loop, the players included a stage driver named Lije Wilson, a sometime miner and more-time prospector named Finnegan Chimes, and a remarkable individual—or so everyone present thought—wearing a chaste black gown with white lacing which did absolutely nothing to conceal the shape of the marvelous figure within. This extraordinary young woman, who couldn't have been more than thirty, with wide-spaced gray eyes, a full, rich mouth, and a head of chestnut hair, could only be described as beautiful—a beauty of the sort that took a man's breath away. And the fact that she was smoking a large Havana cigar did absolutely nothing to detract from her superb body and ravishing looks; indeed, it clearly added to her attractiveness. She was of the sort who could do anything and would still be what she was: an enchantress.

"Mae, I'll see ya," said Clancy O'Rourke, and he pushed chips toward the center of the table.

The lady, taking the cigar out of her gorgeous mouth, nodded in Clancy's direction and pushed a stack of chips forward. "I'll see you, O'Rourke." Her voice was soft and musical, but no one ever missed the streak of authority in it. Mae Dunleary was no person to try pushing. Right now those gray eyes gazed across the table at Clancy O'Rourke, who dropped his own, flushing slightly. It had been said by some writing fellow passing through one of the towns where the lady was at cards that in her eyes lay the innocence of the Devil himself. Those eyes did not change a flicker of their quality now as she raked in her winnings.

It was Three-Fingers Barney Loop's deal. Accepting the deck, he released a soft whistle of pleasure, and, leaning his thick elbows on the green baize tabletop, he fanned the deck open and stared at it thoughtfully. "Ah," he said solemnly, "to study 'the Bible of fifty-two leaves'!" He chuckled. His eyes went around the table. "When two play, my friends, one must lose."

"And when seven play, my friend, six must lose," said Mae sweetly. "Now, let's cut the cackle and get on with the business at hand."

Her words were cool and crisp, neither friendly nor hostile.

Three-Fingers beamed. "I am blessed," he said.

Expertly he shuffled, cut, dealt. He sat back in his chair, sighing, lips pursed, brows lifted, lids lowered to his cards.

"Ah," he sighed. "Another quote: 'Gaming is the son of avarice and the father of despair.'" Three-Fingers folded his hand and placed his cards face-down in front of him.

Mae's face remained impassive. "You should grow up," she said.

Clancy O'Rourke barked out a laugh. "Mae, we love ya!"

"Goddamn it! Let's get to playing cards, you knotheads! God, you can see why Dixie lost the war." But she said this with her voice very low, only for the company directly in the game. The joke brought the players into a shout of laughter. Ollie Wirehouse roared, knocking over his drink. Three-Fingers pounded the table. Lije Wilson, the stage driver, stared in awe at the beautiful creature who had uttered those words. And the onlookers looked at each other.

The players were all in Mae's employ, either in the Lost Mine—left her by Fancy Dan, everyone said, when he succumbed to death from bullets—or in various "side jobs," as she called them, such as the transportation of whiskey, and other matters where efficiency and secrecy were the order of the day.

They were used to her behavior, and her remarks, more or less. She paid well, but she also played cards better than any of them. In fact, Mae was considered a top player in her profession.

At this point the game slowed a little. Following a few more hands, when Clancy slightly increased his bank and the others were about even, Mae picked up a fresh deck.

"Ante a dollar," she said, and took a drag on her cigar, pluming the smoke to the low ceiling of the tight room.

No one voiced an objection, and the money went into the pot.

"Pass," Ollie Wirehouse said.

Mae took a drag on her cigar.

Lije Wilson opened. "I'll make it a dollar for starters."

"I'm in," Clancy said, and he reached for his drink and downed a good wallop.

Mae simply watched her cards and was obviously enjoying her cigar.

Finnegan Chimes, the miner, tossed in a cartwheel.

"Dealer stays." Mae kept her eyes low, waiting.

The room had quieted.

Ollie Wirehouse shoved a dollar toward the center of the table and drew two cards.

"I will accept three of those cards," Clancy said. He looked at the three cards Mae dealt and tossed them into the discard pile. Rubbing his palms together, he settled back in his chair, regarding Mae.

"Well," said Lije Wilson, belching softly into his cards as he studied them. "I'll stay."

"Let's see where you really are," Mae said, her voice challenging.

Color swept into Wilson's thin face. "Table stakes? I'll bet five, then."

Ollie pushed five dollars into the pot. "And make it another five," he said, counting it in cartwheels.

Lije grinned.

"I pass," said Finnegan Chimes.

"And another five," said Lije.

Mae very gently scratched the tip of an ear, which showed beneath her chestnut hair. "I'll call."

"I call your five and raise you five more," Ollie Wirehouse said.

Lije Wilson squinted at his cards, holding them tightly with both hands so that they curved. "See you, I will, and raise you five."

At this moment Mae said sweetly, "I call, and I raise the pot another ten dollars."

Lije's mouth fell open, while across Ollie's face swept astonishment and then pique.

"Damn it," Ollie said. "Letting that last one go by. Falling for that old one. Betcha got four of a kind, by golly!"

"There's only one way to find out, boys," Mae said, and her eyes held a wicked look.

"We'll soon see, then," Ollie said. "Lije . . ." His voice was grim.

"I'm in," Lije said, and he leaned forward.

Mae's face was without any expression, except possibly that of innocence, as she spread four kings and an ace on the baize and raked in the final pot.

Someone stood up and turned down the lamp, which was beginning to smoke, and the smell of coal oil was filling the room.

The poker players sat in their chairs for a few

moments longer. And so Mae had wiped them out
again. But they were not crestfallen. They had all
enjoyed the game. Each one of them had enjoyed
simply being with Mae.

It was just at this restrained moment, when the
players were loosening into their drinks and smokes,
that one of the bartenders appeared on the scene. The
group of onlookers opened a slight passageway for
him, and he approached, his eyes on Mae, who was
studying the ash on the end of her cigar. The bartender's name was Cy. He was bald, totally, and he
always looked worried. As now. He waited until the
lady at the table raised her eyes to take him in.

"What is it, Cy? Time?"

"Yes, Mae." And he lifted his worried eyes toward the ceiling.

"Everybody's there?"

"Everybody."

"Gentlemen, excuse me." And she stood up. The
seated men rose with her and stood while she followed the bartender as the onlookers parted to make
a wider passage.

Eyes followed, and along with those eyes, silence. Nobody uttered a sound as the woman who
had again stripped them—so deftly, with such exper-
tise—crossed the room to the stairs leading to the
floor above. Everyone saw that while she was composed and serious, there yet seemed to be a sort of
smile behind her lips, her eyes. None of them could
have defined that expression, but all felt it.

John Slocum, who had been watching the group
as he stood at the bar, noticed it. And indeed, as the

lady raised her head a little, her eyes caught his. And he felt something go through him.

"That's the boss." It was Clarence Roller speaking as he drew up next to Slocum.

Slocum didn't take his eyes off the woman. "She's got to be more than just that," he said. And then as he caught her eye for a fleeting second, he gave an imperceptible nod. Her eyes moved away, and he knew it had registered.

Slocum watched her as she went up the stairs, holding her long skirt in one hand so that she wouldn't trip. She had a very straight back, he noted, but what he really appreciated was how she didn't walk across the room but simply moved.

After a moment Roller said, "What do you make of this parade that's being planned?"

"Somebody's running for something, I'd say." Slocum's eyes were on the stairs. "What's her name?"

"Dunleary."

"Dunleary," Slocum said, musing on the name. "Sounds familiar."

"Familiar? You know it? You've heard it before?" Roller turned his granite face away from the room and looked directly at Slocum.

"Puts me in mind of that name you said, and I heard it somewhere else, I believe."

"Hmm," said Roller.

"Dunroodie."

"What're you thinking?"

"That it's a coincidence. Hell, there's MacPherson and MacDonald."

Roller said, "In this line of work a man can go

crazy trying to pin the tail on the donkey."

"She got a mister?"

"Dead. I been told."

"What about Fancy Dan Diamond?"

"The lady is free, as far as I hear tell. He's dead too. You're interested, huh."

"Right now, only so far as this business with Rumpel and his bunch."

"Good," said Roller. "A man's got to keep his eye on the job at such times. Afraid, though, I can't help you much. I am also trying to find the handle on this outhouse door."

Slocum turned suddenly, picked up his glass, and said, "Let's get that table over there." And without waiting for a response he walked through the crowd to the vacated table at the far side of the room. Roller could do nothing else but follow.

When they were seated, Slocum said, "Roller, I want to know what you're up to. You've been *talking* straight to me, but you haven't *been* straight. You get me? You get the difference?"

The lanky man nodded, his face still gray and grave. "Excepting I did tell you the way of it. I am looking for Cotton Dunroodie, and his trail led me to Rumpel. Rumpel hired me to keep a eye on you. Of course I never let on to Rumpel why I was hunting Dunroodie, and I figured it'd be a good way for me to watch Rumpel, since he seemed to be a connection—that is, working for him."

"Neat. But who is Dunroodie? There's something real familiar about that name, but I can't find it."

"Reckon I better give you the straight of it, Slocum." Roller lowered his voice and leaned forward, but with his eyes looking about the room.

"That's what I've been suggesting," Slocum said dryly.

"I haven't laid it out before this on account of I wasn't sure of anything. Wasn't sure of yourself, like you wasn't of me neither."

"C'mon, Roller, get to the point."

"I'm just looking to see if there's anybody about here who might be interested in our conversation."

"That feller yonder by the faro game," Slocum said. "But he can't hear us. I've been watching him."

"About a year ago, a man named Kyle Creamer escaped jail in New Orleans. Creamer was a riverboat gambler, or so it said on his record. Except he was more than that. Actually his name was—is— Cotton Pettijohn Dunroodie, and he had been—"

But Slocum interrupted him, slapping the palm of his hand down on the table. "That's it! Pettijohn! You're going to tell me he rode with Quantrill!"

"And with the Kansas Jayhawkers, and a whole lot more," Roller said. "You know him?"

"Let's say I've heard of him. I knew there was something familiar in that name when you first said it. Yes! He was Cotton D. Pettijohn. People always said he kept the 'D.' in his name, and they referred to him that way, with that middle initial. Funny. . ."

"What? What's funny?"

"How some men change their names but still don't quite change it. Not completely."

Roller nodded. "Dunroodie, you may or may not know, is said to be grease with his gun, and accurate. And he's a murderer—that's what they were holding him for in New Orleans." He leaned forward, pushing his glass out of the way as he brought his hands down onto the table. And now his tone was confiding. "You knew him, did you, Slocum?"

"Roller, what did I just tell you a couple of minutes ago?"

Clarence Roller shrugged, leaned back, and said, "Forgot."

"Now I have a question," Slocum said.

Roller's forehead wrinkled.

"Who hired you to find Dunroodie? Or do I need to ask?"

"You don't need to ask. The law."

"What are you doing about finding him?"

"He's said to have been heading northwest with an immigrant train. Well, I went through St. Joseph and a few other places of departure for the west, and not a trace, though I was wondering if he might've been with those three carnival wagons. He could still be, for the matter of that. Not hard to hide a man, if there's cooperation."

Slocum nodded. "That is so."

"You hear anything, let me know," Roller said.

"You got a description? What he looks like?"

Roller pursed his lips, blinking slowly in thought. "Kind of hard to describe. Tall, lean, fast, in his thirties. That's what I've been told. There's no photograph of him, least that anybody knows of. About six feet." His face twisted into a wry grin. "Could be like you or myself." He stood up, and Slocum regarded him quietly. "We'll keep on it, then," Roller said.

"Rumpel ever seen him?"

"He said no."

"And do you figure Rumpel wants to locate him so's he can hire him?"

"That sounds likely."

"Or kill him? Maybe there's more likely. Maybe Dunroodie's been in this country."

"That sounds possible," Clarence Roller said. He lifted his Stetson hat and set it down on his head again in a fresh way. "How do you see that, Slocum?"

"I'd say Rumpel might likely figure on both."

"Both." Roller pursed his lips at that, lifted his forehead, and nodded a couple of times. "Hunh."

"Liken he's figuring with you and me," Slocum said.

In the big room upstairs at the Lost Mine Saloon, which was part of Mae Dunleary's living quarters, the lady sat in her favorite position at one end of a horsehair sofa while her two visitors sat in easy chairs, also of horsehair.

"My dear, it is a delight to see you again," Ralph Rumpel was saying as he poured a second round of champagne.

"I can only repeat what has just been said," said Hector Kinsolving, adjusting his weight somewhat on his chair. His trousers were feeling too tight, especially around the waist and crotch.

"I hope you're satisfied with the way things are going, Ralph," Mae said, and lifted her glass.

"Thus far, my dear. Thus far. One must not count one's eggs before they're hatched, of course. But things are looking good. I must say." And he raised his glass to hers, while Kinsolving followed suit.

"That sparkly is the best I've had in a long time," Mae said.

"Definitely not for the redskins," laughed Rumpel.

"Or anyone else," added Kinsolving.

Rumpel put down his glass on the small table beside his chair. "I have your report. And I am pleased. Now we need to get moving with our parade. Hector has everything running smoothly. Isn't that right, Hector?"

"Correct." And Hector Kinsolving beamed, thinking not only that the champagne was superb but that the creature on the sofa was worth her weight in gold ten times over. But then he saw her looking at him in a way that he took to be suspicious, and he forced himself to think of something else.

"The Indians," Rumpel was saying, "are going to make trouble. The hope is that it will not be very big trouble, but only just enough—encouraged by the whiskey—to frighten everyone."

"And not more than the vigilantes can handle, I assume," Mae said.

"Flanagan and his men have their orders. Flanagan will personally lead one band of vigilantes, and Hooligan another." Rumpel rubbed his puffy palms together.

"The risk will be minimal, I gather," Kinsolving said.

"The risk will hardly exist. The men have orders not to kill, but only to restrain. After all, we don't want an Indian war. We are in the business of restoring order and keeping it. We are safeguarding the citizens of Cold Rock and indeed this large section of the territory."

"Ralph, you're going to make a very fine delegate," said Mae, and she lifted her glass again. "I toast you and your immediate appointment as delegate for the Territory of Montana!"

They drank.

"We might open that second bottle," Rumpel said.

"Good idea," said Kinsolving. "There's a good aftertaste to that brand."

But Mae was not smiling. Her face was serious as she watched Rumpel open the second bottle of champagne. And when the cork popped loudly, she didn't change her expression. "What about this man Slocum?" she said. "And that other one, Roller?"

"You've seen them, have you?" Rumpel asked, sitting down again.

She nodded.

"They are insurance," Rumpel said. "They have and will have their uses to, uh, the enterprise." He smiled, and drank heartily.

"And Gallup?" Kinsolving asked.

"Gallup has played his part admirably and will continue to do so," Rumpel said.

"You're going to have to elect a sheriff," Mae said suddenly. "You can't run things with a vigilante committee forever."

"I can while there's trouble."

"Yes, but we can't go on making trouble for the next five or ten years, my friend," she said sweetly.

"Of course. But of course. Flanagan can be our sheriff. We'll just have to find someone he can run against so the people are satisfied with themselves.

That will be easy." He beamed at them, feeling, he had to admit, like royalty—or, that is to say, as he put it to himself, power granting favors and enlightenment to those in need. But he felt the woman's eyes on him.

"And the cattle business?" she said. "Is that still going to be?"

"But of course, of course, of course. We've shown that a herd can get through. The trail has been blazed. Who knows? We might be able to hire Slocum again as a sort of permanent drover. He really did something getting that herd up here."

"Others might not be so fortunate," Mae pointed out.

"The trail has been blazed. I tell you, my dear, a year from now it will be easy as eating apple pie."

"Once the railroad spur is in, we can ship direct from Cold Rock," Kinsolving said.

"How will that affect Hitch Town," Mae asked, "taking that business away from them? I mean, that's what they live on now, the fact that they're a shipping point. I still don't see how you're going to get the Union Pacific to drop Hitch Town and build a spur out here. And besides, why does Cold Rock have to be the shipping point? Hitch Town isn't all that far away."

Rumpel was grinning. "But that's just the point, my dear. You have missed some of the beauty of my plan. Don't you see that when I am delegate I shall have power, I shall have means of, so to say, quiet, even silent persuasion. In a word, Hitch Town will be within my purview."

"Ralph, I don't quite understand yet how that part

will work. How can you make Cold Rock the shipping point if the U.P. spur now goes only as far as
Hitch Town?" Hector Kinsolving put down his glass
of champagne and regarded Ralph Rumpel with a
questioning look all over his face.

"But don't you see"—Rumpel leaned forward on
his knees—"the two of you? Don't you see that nobody has to do anything? Because shortly after I become delegate for the Territory of Montana, I shall
see to it that Hitch Town will be—and will assuredly
want to be—a part of Cold Rock." Rumpel lifted his
glass. "We should get on with more planning for the
parade. But first, shall we drink to what I just said?"

"About Hitch Town?" Mae asked, with a smile
just touching the corners of her mouth.

"Yes," Rumpel said. "Yes, indeed. About Hitch
Town and all the other things. Our plans—maybe I
could be so bold as to say my plans, but with your
very much needed assistance and abilities—are only
beginning to come to fruition. We are at the dawn of
an era, in fact."

This time they didn't open another bottle. There
was plenty of time for that later. During and after the
parade. And there was work to be done now.

Both men were feeling the presence of Mae Dunleary for a long time after their meeting ended. But
Ralph Rumpel had the satisfaction of knowing that
he could—and he surely would—satisfy himself
with Melissa, his beloved, who surely had to be as
capable as any Mae Dunleary. Shouldn't she? As for
Kinsolving, he had his wife of so many years expecting him home in the evening. Not that Hector was a

henpecked husband, but he knew how good it was to know where his bread was buttered.

As for Mae, the lady in question, she found herself wondering about the tall, broad-shouldered man with the raven-black hair and the bright green eyes who had looked at her with a gaze that she could actually feel touching her body. She had never had that experience before. It was kind of spooky, she decided, as she came back downstairs from her quarters and reentered the saloon. Spooky. But also something she thought she'd definitely like to look into.

She had just returned to the room where earlier she had wiped out her little band of business associates and had seated herself at the round baize-top table to deal herself some solitaire when there came a knock at the door.

"Come in," she said, without looking up.

The door opened, and the bald-headed bartender was there. "Mae, there's some feller at the bar says he wants to talk to you. I told him you was busy, but he was the kind . . . well, he was sort of insistent."

"Big fellow?"

"Big. Yes."

"Black hair."

"Yeah, that's right."

"Green eyes."

"You know him, then."

"I just don't know his name."

"I don't neither, Mae. But he's waiting."

10

Slocum had decided that it was time to play his cards or get out of the game. No sense, he knew, in just sitting staring the spots off those pasteboards. He was going over just that when the woman named Mae appeared at his side.

"Man said you were looking for me, mister. Wanted to ask something, did you?"

"I did." He answered her slowly, his eyes taking in the full bust, the throat leading down to what could only be a marvelous pair of breasts. It was obvious to his practiced eye that she was wearing a minimum of clothing beneath that long black gown. Her shoulders, her arms, and her hands were in perfect proportion to the rest of her body—at least to what was visible of it. But he knew that the invisible had to be of equal or even superior quality. She was wearing a musky perfume that he had never smelled before. "That's nice perfume you got there, lady."

"Glad you like it." Her smile was mostly in her eyes, though he could see the corners of her mouth twitching. "What did you want to ask me? The brand of perfume?"

"I didn't want to ask much. At least I think I've

about forgotten what I wanted to ask you."

"I don't know that I believe that. I've heard of you, Mr. Slocum. You don't come off as the type of man who forgets anything."

"How about yourself? Do you forget things?"

"Give me a try, and then you'll know."

It was then he took a shot in the dark. "Remember a man named Cotton Dunroodie?"

"Never heard of him. Should I have?"

"Just asking. Took a wild shot at it."

"Why are we standing here? Why not sit down?"

"Can I buy you a drink?"

She nodded to the bartender as they moved off to a table in the corner of the room. Slocum was fully aware of the room watching them, and he knew he was making himself a possible target. But he'd gotten to the point where he felt the need to take a step. To move the situation. He had the very strong feeling that things were coming to a climax, and that if he didn't make a move to open things up he was going to somehow miss out.

They sat down, and the bartender brought drinks.

"I understand you own this place," he said.

"So you figure I meet a lot of people and would maybe know this man you mention. What's his name?"

"Well, actually, he's got two names. Cotton Dunroodie, and Cotton D. Pettijohn."

"I might have heard the name someplace, but I can't remember. Is it all that important?"

"It's settled. Let's get onto something really important."

"Like what?"

"Like when are you off duty? I'd like to get to know you better."

"I'm off duty now."

"So it's my turn to buy the drinks." And he signaled the bartender. He could still feel the room watching them. Turning back to her he said, "I watched some of your game a while back. You're pretty good."

"I'm damn good, Mr. Slocum."

"Maybe with those players. But I did admire the way you buried that fourth king on your last hand. Remember? The hand where you let the last bet go by and then you clobbered the boys."

"You're pretty sharp."

"Just habit. I take it as a hobby to notice things." He was looking into her eyes, wondering whether they were really velvet, or whether his mind was playing him tricks.

"What would you like to do?" she asked. "Another drink?"

"A little privacy might help," he said.

"As the proprietor of the Lost Mine, I don't indulge in intimacies with the customers."

"I'm not a customer," Slocum said. "I'm a guest."

"Who invited you?"

"Why, you did."

"Did I?"

"Yes, indeed."

She looked a little flustered then, but he knew she was only putting it on. She was smiling at him, and he felt his loins stirring.

It was at this point that someone shouted through

the batwing doors, "Somebody get Doc. Hank Larrabee's been beat up bad!"

"I have to see to that," Slocum said, standing up quickly.

"I'll be around," Mae said.

And he was out the door, running down to the livery, assuming that was the place where the beating had happened. And as he approached he could see the crowd gathering. All at once he felt the anger coming. And he knew that he was going to even it for that old man, no matter how long it might take.

Doc Fable was at hand, and by the time Slocum got to the livery Hank was just conscious.

"My kid found him lying there," a man with a short beard said to the crowd. "All beat up he was. I sent Tommy for the doc and tried to carry Hank inside to lie him down somewheres. Then Pop come and helped me." He turned to Pop Tilghman, who owned the livery, for confirmation.

"Hank was out of it. I mean out of it. I dunno who beat him up, but I lay my hands on the sonofabitch he's gonna wish I'd kill him fast, which I won't."

The man was shaking with outrage, and so was the crowd that had gathered, save the children, who were simply thunderstruck.

Slocum pushed in close. Hank was barely conscious. His eyes wandered about, but he obviously couldn't focus. His beard had blood in it, and there was a cut along his forehead.

"Who did it, Hank?"

"Leave him be now," Doc said. "He don't know where he is, or anything. You'll just confuse him.

We'll talk to him when he's got himself rested."

Some people offered their homes for him, but a widow named Hester Glebe offered to take him into her spare room. Slocum went along and stayed until the old man was safely in bed, with clean sheets and attention from Mrs. Glebe and Doc Fable.

"I'd like to talk to him, Doc, when you think it would be all right," Slocum said, taking Fable aside. "I want to find out who did it."

It developed that Hester Glebe had two grown sons, and she volunteered both of them to remain on guard during the old man's stay in the house.

Slocum was greatly relieved to hear it. "I'll be about if there's anything that I can do, Mrs. Glebe," he told her.

She was a small, thoroughly capable woman, and he could see she wasn't anybody to rub the wrong way, and this also made him feel good that Hank was in her hands.

When he left the house, Hank was still not talking and was still obviously not very sure where he was. But he was ready for sleep. Doc Fable gave him medicine for that.

And so Slocum decided to take in the parade, but to keep an eye on the house at the same time. At the parade it might be possible to pick up some kind of lead as to what the attack had been about. Why had someone picked on Hank Larrabee? Was it just random violence? He found that hard to believe. Did somebody think the old man knew something he shouldn't know? It was the only answer Slocum could come up with. For Hank didn't have anything worth stealing. Not as far as he knew. He was just an

old man with his memories. But he did like to talk.
Everybody knew that. He talked to himself, he talked
to the animals, to the sky, and if any person happened to be around, he talked to them.

Maybe this time somebody had been around who
didn't like what Old Hank was saying.

Pretty soon after the sun had left the sky, the main
street began to fill with people. The streetlights, such
as they were, went on, but mostly light shone forth
from the saloons and gaming halls, the How-Do Eatery, which always stayed open late, and the cribs.
Soon the stars appeared in the vast sky. And in no
time at all the street was packed with people and the
boardwalks were overflowing.

The crowd was noisy, milling about, excited, and
filled with anticipation. The talk was loud, inter-
spersed with shouts and singing rivaling the sounds
of the crowded saloons and dance halls.

Ralph Rumpel and his committee had worked out
the plan with great care. Ralph had not been a riverboat gambler and a shill and a medicine hawker and a
bunco artist all those years without understanding the
various ways of manipulating people—people as individuals, or people in groups or crowds.

Early on, the vigilante members began to filter
into the crowd. Gamblers, also aligned to Rumpel's
cause, left their gaming tables to mingle with the citizens of Cold Rock.

The astute Rumpel, aided by the provocative and
persuasive Mae, had arranged certain groups in cou-
ples; the purpose being first of all to support each
other and at the same time to talk up Ralph Rumpel

and his plan for the territory, and especially for Cold Rock. A petition would be passed later in the evening and the names sent to Washington by special courier.

This shilling they did in conversations with one another, so loud that everyone could hear in the vicinity, and now and then they would address some stranger with a question about the governing of the territory, using the other person's response as an opening to sell Ralph Rumpel. The fine art of the shill was right there for anyone to see, Slocum noted with a certain amusement.

All at once a tremendous shouting down at the far end of the street triggered a roar along the crowded boardwalks, swiftly augmented by the banging of a big bass drum.

"Here they come!"

And as Slocum reached a place from which he had a clear view of the proceedings, he could feel the crowd stiffening, then churning.

The big drum was even louder now, and accompanied by a fife plus some fiddles and a pair of banjos. An ancient citizen known as Lanky Leonard blew on his cornet, his cheeks round and hard as balls, as he marched in tune to his own music—which, however, wasn't always the same as that played by his companions.

There were some clowns, there was a coyote on a chain, several dogs, a Texas longhorn wearing a placard, which was bothering him a good bit and he was spooking about, frightening people, but three men were keeping him in line. Fortunately for the spectators the longhorn wore hobbles, and his horns had been capped with metal and cloth. There was a tumbler, and there was a juggler. And there were children running in and out of the parade, which also consisted of the usual riders on their mounts, ready to corral the entire parade if it got out of hand, or the crowd, if that should become necessary. These were the vigilantes under the gimlet-eyed care of Boyd Flanagan and his men.

Smack-dab in the very center of the procession, under a huge Texas hat, rode Ralph Rumpel in a spring wagon drawn by a pair of spanking bays. He was dressed in black broadcloth, with an enormous red sash running from his right shoulder diagonally across his chest to his waist and also across his back. He was beaming, waving at the crowd, blowing kisses to the children, and even as the cheering grew into greater swells, removing the huge white hat and waving it.

The exciting firelight from the torches on the sweating faces of the parading men, the thudding drum, the clashing cymbals, the darting in and out of the children with their firecrackers, which they shamelessly tossed with shrieks and giggles of excitement into the ranks of the marchers—all added to the hammering excitement.

At a certain unpropitious moment someone tossed a firecracker at the feet of Ralph Rumpel's bays, both of whom began to rear, and it looked as though they would bolt. But Slocum, who was only a few feet away, sprang off the boardwalk and grabbed both horses by their chin straps. He was pulled off his feet but held on while the crowd gasped and Flanagan, the vigilante leader, shouted orders for the parade to stop.

Slocum calmed the bays, then calmed Ralph Rumpel, who was now doing his best to put a good face on the terror that had gripped him. Soon all was well, and again the drum began to beat, the fiddles to fiddle, and the cornet to blow, and the parade moved on, finally coming to a halt outside the frame schoolhouse. Here the man who was the center of the whole affair was helped down, and with his feet firmly on the ground, he stepped up onto the boardwalk outside the door of the schoolhouse.

"My friends, I shall be brief. First, I wish to thank you one and all for your support of myself and my associates, who have—and I say this with, I trust, pardonable pride—brought peace to our troubled town, and with the arrival of our first herd of longhorns, a promise of prosperity. I see Cold Rock as a community that will grow. And I promise you now that should I be designated the delegate for the Montana Territory, I shall perform my duties with all my heart and soul. I shall of course put an immediate stop to the selling of whiskey to the Indian tribes, and shall continue to rid the country of the road agents, cattle rustlers, horse thieves, and other and all criminal elements. I shall urge Army support in the containment of the Indians on their reservations. This, again, will be a part of my campaign against the whiskey peddlers, those demons who purvey the Devil's drink to those wild and very dangerous savages."

There was more, but Slocum had heard enough. The parade was over. The drinking would surely go on. But he wanted time to think and piece things together.

As he walked down to the Widow Glebe's house he wondered where Roller was. He hadn't seen him in a while.

To his great surprise when he knocked on Mrs. Glebe's door, it was opened by Norah, the girl whose last name he did not remember but whose face and body and willingness he would not soon forget.

"What are you doing here?" he asked.

"I'm helping with Mr. Larrabee," she said. "The doctor said somebody was needed, and I happened to overhear him." She offered him a seat in the living room. "Mrs. Glebe has gone to bed. The boys are in the kitchen trying to repair something. I don't know what."

"Is it too late?" Slocum asked. "I saw the light on and I just wanted to drop by to see how he is."

"He's asleep," she said. And then, "A man came by to see him. He said he was a friend."

Instantly Slocum felt something grab him inside. "Who was it? What was his name?"

She was instantly caught by his tone of voice and showed her alarm. "I—I, yes, it was... well, he didn't give me his name actually, but he was someone I've seen around."

"Tell me what he looked like."

"He was that man who came with all those riders after the storm and the Indians."

"Flanagan!"

"I think that was his name."

"What did he want?"

"He said he wanted to know how Mr. Larrabee

was. I didn't let him inside. He just wanted to ask how he was."

Slocum leaned toward her, leaning on his knees as he sat on the edge of the sofa. "Listen, you're sure he didn't go in."

"Oh, I'm sure. The doctor told me nobody must go in except you and Mrs. Glebe and myself—oh, and Tom and Miller, her boys."

"How long did he stay?"

"Maybe a few minutes. Why? Is something wrong?"

"What did he ask you?"

"Only how Mr. Larrabee was. Whether he was awake."

"Did he ask whether he'd said anything?"

She considered that a moment and then said, "Why, yes, he did. And I said he said a few words, and the man—Mr. Flanagan—asked what were they. I said I didn't remember."

"And then he left?"

She nodded, her face tense now. "Did I do something wrong?"

"No. Not at all. Tell me, though, did Hank say anything to you, even something you might not have understood? You can tell me, you can trust me."

She thought a moment, her forehead creased slightly, and then her face cleared. "No, there's nothing."

"Nothing about, say, the mines, or anybody's names."

"No."

"Does the name Cotton Dunroodie mean anything to you?"

She shook her head. "I don't know that name." She clasped her hands together on her lap. "I—I feel funny. I wish you would tell me what's wrong. Is there something wrong?"

"I think everything's all right. I just want to be sure. Now can I take a look at him? I just want to see how he is. I won't disturb him."

She stood up. "Yes, of course."

She lighted a coal-oil lamp and carried it to the door of the room where Hank Larrabee had been put. The old man was asleep. They could hear his breathing the moment they opened his door.

Slocum handed the lamp to the girl while he studied the battered face lying on the pillow. "Were his pockets emptied, Norah?"

"It's all on the bureau there."

A timepiece, some chewing tobacco, a clasp knife. Nothing of any particular interest. A few coins, an old button, and a roll of string. Slocum picked up the button.

He stood for a moment listening to the old man's breathing, and then he touched the girl's arm and they went back to the front room.

"Thanks for giving me your time," he said.

"Thank you for coming by."

"You keep that door locked. The front door, and the back."

She was looking at him intently now. "There is something wrong, isn't there?"

He looked at her as though trying to make up his mind, and then he said, "Why would anyone want to beat him up like that? Why didn't they just kill him? Of course, they might have been interrupted. That's what Doc thought. But I don't know. Maybe they were beating him to get some information. What do you think?"

"I'm afraid I'm not very good at thinking about things like that," Norah said. "It's just . . . it just is so horrible that anyone would do that to another person, and to an old man like that."

"Let me say hello to the boys," Slocum said.

She smiled at him then, her face brightening. And then she walked to a bedroom door and opened it. "Gentlemen, this is Mr. John Slocum. He's a friend of Mr. Larrabee. Tom and Miller Glebe."

They were young men, open-faced, and he just said hello and goodbye, and then he and Norah were back in the living room.

"I'm glad you met them," she said.

"I'll go along now. I've got a lot of thinking to do. But you make sure they stay with you in the house."

She walked him to the door. And then suddenly she was in his arms. "Hold me. Please hold me. I'm afraid. I'm sorry, I'm not very brave. But this, what happened, it's so awful!"

"I can stay here with you, if you like."

"No, thank you. It would be better not. Mrs. Glebe is here. And the boys. But maybe you could come tomorrow." She was looking up into his eyes, and suddenly he realized how much prettier she was than Mae Dunleary.

He kissed her then, and they clung together.

He spent the night in the livery. It felt good being there with his pony and the other horses. And it was a good place to think. Also, he had the feeling that he was being watched, and he didn't want to be a sitting target in his room at the hotel.

Suddenly he was wide awake. He lay on his bedroll, his hand on the butt of his six-gun, listening. What was it? A pack rat? Could be. Only he'd heard pack rats in the night a lot of times and didn't feel like this about it. He listened.

And then he realized it wasn't any sound in the livery, or even outside. It was something inside him.

The whole game that Rumpel was playing was so clear now. The game of making your own enemy so that you could knock him down and then play the hero, the savior. Setting up the straw man and downing him. A game as old as the mountains. And people fell for it. Create the problem for everybody and then come in strong and solve it and they ate out of your hand. So simple!

Well, that was clear, but he still felt something missing. Rumpel after all was going to get his position as delegate or he wasn't. That would work out one way or another. People would fall for it or not. But there was something more to the whole game. He knew it. He knew it in his bones, in his blood.

For it was all, in a sense, on the up-and-up. The cattle drive, with Cold Rock becoming a big depot for the Texas herds. That was sure. The Indians stirred up and the road agents working so that the vigilantes could come in and save everybody. Any bunco artist worthy of the name learned that one in the cradle. There was nothing new under the sun; only the way it was sold was what could be new.

All right, then. So where did Old Hank Larrabee

fit in? Or was that just an accident, a coincidence? And what about himself? What about Roller? Well, it made sense for a man like Rumpel to have some good men working for him. The Boyd Flanagans, the Clyde Hooligans, and all the rest of that sort were unreliable. They couldn't control their tempers for one thing. Look at that fool Link Rudabaugh. But Rumpel knew how to play people off against each other.

Slocum thought about that now, lying there on his bedroll, half listening to a pack rat scampering about nearby, another chewing something at the far end of the barn. Who was Rumpel trying to play him against? Roller? Who was Roller? And who was Cotton Dunroodie? Cotton Pettijohn. He remembered Pettijohn now. He'd been one of Bloody Bill Anderson's men. A murderous sonofabitch, like all of that bunch. But—Dunroodie?

He had made up that story to Roller about knowing somebody named Cotton Pettijohn who had changed his name to Pettijohn Dunroodie, or something like that. He had said it simply to get Roller to say more. But Roller had accepted what he'd said so easily about Cotton D. Pettijohn and about how men sometimes weren't able to change their names completely, and often kept part of the old name.

But he could get no further with it, and he was beginning to feel sleepy. It was getting close to dawn. He could feel it. He dozed, still half awake, lying just under the surface of an awakened state, like he did on the trail. For he did feel the sense of danger this night. He had felt it in the Glebe house with Norah, and he felt it right here in the livery.

And then for a moment his thoughts went toward Mae, that luscious creature who ran the Lost Mine and played poker like the very best he'd seen. Mae. And he remembered how when he was with Norah earlier this evening he had felt so strongly how much more beautiful she was than the fabulous Mae Dunleary.

And then all at once, like a star dropping out of the sky, he had it. And he was wide awake. But he continued to lie there, fitting all the pieces together. And when that was done, he slept. He slept for a very short while, but he slept peacefully.

11

He was up before dawn and waiting for the How-Do Eatery to open so he could have coffee. Then he walked down to the Glebe house.

Everybody was up and they were glad to see him. The boys, Miller and Tom, had already gone to work. Even Hank Larrabee was awake, though not feeling too chipper. Still, he recognized Slocum, and even managed to joke a bit.

"Didn't believe me when I told you this was a wild town, did you, young feller?" And he cackled.

"Hank, who did it? Who beat you?"

"If I knowed that, d'you think I'd be lying here, goddamn it. I'd be after that sonofabitch, I mean right now!"

"I guess you would at that, by golly," said Slocum with a big grin. "Tell me, did whoever it was take anything? Papers, money, a timepiece, anything?"

"I don't have anything to be took." He nodded at the bedside table. "That's my worldly possessions. I am a millionaire. Got more air in my pockets than the president of the Union Pacific."

"Boy, I'm glad to see you're feeling better. But you stay in bed today and rest."

"I will if I feel like it. Later, I'm going out to have a look-see. You never know. I might smell the sonofabitch."

"Was it one man or more?"

"Dunno."

"Do you have any notion why?"

The old man gave him a funny look then. "Sure I know why, Slocum. But that's—what I just this minute said—that's between you an' me."

"You going to tell me what it is?"

He screwed up his face then, as though trying to remember something. "Nope. Not today."

"You stay in bed. You hear me?"

"You my mother?"

"No. I'm just the feller who's going to try to fix it so's you can keep whatever you've got in your head to stay there."

"That's your business, Slocum."

"And yours. Remember that. You don't have to tell me anything, but we're still partners whether you like it or not. Now shut up and go to sleep. There's somebody at the door." And he walked out, closing the door behind him.

It was Boyd Flanagan at the door, along with two of his men. The girl had opened the door just slightly, but they were almost on the point of pushing in.

"We're the Vigilance Committee in town here, miss. That's to say, we're the law. And we would like to talk to Hank about his accident."

Slocum heard Mrs. Glebe moving around in the kitchen. "You men stay right where you are!" he said.

"Get out of the way, Slocum!" Flanagan pushed the door open, thrusting Norah back. "We're here for the law. Don't you try to stop us."

"You're here for Rumpel," Slocum said. "Norah, go into the kitchen with Mrs. Glebe."

"The girl stays here, Slocum," snapped Flanagan.

"Flanagan, there are three of you and one of me. The girl is going in the kitchen. Norah—go."

Flanagan grinned as the girl walked past Slocum and out of the room. "Pretty tough, ain't you, Slocum?"

"I am what I am, Flanagan. You ready?"

"Mr. Rumpel don't want no violence."

"Then get out of here."

At that moment a familiar voice broke into the scene. "What's going on here? Let me in."

"Come on in, Roller. I been wondering what happened to you." And in that split second Slocum knew that Roller knew and he drew and fired.

Roller took the slug right between the eyes. His own gun fell unfired to the floor.

"You men hold it!" snapped Slocum. "Come on in and drop your belts. Unbuckle, I am saying right now."

They did as he ordered.

He had heard the startled cry coming from the kitchen, and now he called out, "It's all right, Mrs. Glebe. It's all right."

"What the hell's the matter with you, Slocum!" Flanagan suddenly roared out. "What the hell you shot Roller for!"

"It wasn't Roller I shot, mister. It was Cotton

Dunroodie. Rumpel isn't the only one who can pull that bunco game."

He heard the door open off to his side then, but he didn't take his eyes away from the three men he had covered, even though they were now unarmed. Slocum had no wish to be one of those men who remembered too late that they had forgotten about hideouts.

"Come in, Hank."

And there was Old Hank Larrabee standing there in his longhandles with the trapdoor in the behind sagging like laundry hanging on a clothesline.

"Norah! Mrs. Glebe! Come in!"

It was Mrs. Glebe who gave the ladylike gasp when she saw Mr. Henry Larrabee in his BVDs.

"Norah, collect those guns."

"Slocum, the Vigilance Committee is gonna see you about this," said Boyd Flanagan, but his attempted bravado was pretty weak. He evidently realized it, for he tried to make up for it by asking, "How did you figger Roller was Dunroodie?"

"Here's that button that's missing off his jacket. Hank had it. Probably grabbed it when Dunroodie beat him up. There's more to it, but you buggers haul out of here. You'll leave your guns. And you'll tell Mr. Ralph Rumpel something."

They had started to move, but now they stopped to hear what Slocum had to say.

Slocum cut his eye at Hank, who didn't seem to mind it at all that he was standing there with his trapdoor unbuttoned for all the world, and the two women, to see. Not that they were looking. Mrs. Glebe was staring in horror at the scene on the floor of her living room. Norah was staring at John Slocum.

"I'll get some people to clean up, Mrs. Glebe," Slocum said, not having any idea what he should be saying to the poor woman at such a time.

"What do you want to tell Mr. Rumpel?" Flanagan said. And right now he was not at all like the old bullyboy that everyone in Cold Rock and Fort Worth and a number of other places knew.

"You can tell him what happened here. And you can tell him if he wants to be a delegate or whatever it is, I don't give a damn. But you will tell him that I am partners with Mr. Henry Larrabee, and if anyone —I say anyone—messes with this man, he'll be messing with me. Now git! And send—no, don't send. You take Dunroodie with you. Then you can send men to clean this place for Mrs. Glebe."

But before anyone could make a move to follow Slocum's orders, a new voice came from the open doorway.

"Mr. Slocum, I'm sorry to cut in on your heroic efforts, but there is the law here in Cold Rock, and I—"

"I am the law in Cold Rock, Rumpel. Do you understand me? I will be the law here until a United States marshal is sent. The request will go in this morning. I say, do you understand me?"

Rumpel had walked further in now and saw the body on the floor. He looked at Slocum. "I understand you, Slocum," he said wearily. Then he somehow pulled himself together. "Am I under arrest, Marshal, or whatever you are?"

"Not as long as you don't leave town."

"You've got nothing on me, Slocum."

"The new marshal will decide that. I don't particularly care. Did you happen to hear what I said about myself and Hank Larrabee? I want to be sure you heard that."

"I did, Slocum. And I expect half the town heard it. Anyhow"—and he straightened a little—"you'll have to admit, my friend, that Ralph Rumpel does know something about hiring the best." He took a step toward the dead man. "Obviously he wasn't a very good selection."

"He did his best," Slocum said. "Maybe he got a little rusty in that New Orleans jail. You know, I didn't mind him—Roller—until he beat up on Hank. I guess gold can twist any man."

"I'd like to ask you one thing, Slocum, if I may."

Slocum said nothing.

"How did you discover that Roller was Dunroodie?"

Slocum holstered his gun then, which he had simply been holding easy in his hand. "Rumpel, don't you know that the best bunco artists and second dealers never—but never—give away the tricks of their trade." His grin was wicked as he looked directly at Ralph Rumpel. "I will tell you, Rumpel. I figured out Dunroodie—and his wife, or sister, I'm not certain which she is, Dunleary—the same way I figured your game wasn't cattle—it was power, political power."

"So what's wrong with that, mister?"

"Nothing. But the gold that Hank Larrabee knew about, the extra strip that he used to talk about, mostly to himself. That was his business. It was—

and still is—Hank's business. And not yours, and not Dunroodie's. It is Hank Larrabee's."

"But he can't remember!" Rumpel suddenly shouted. "Can't you understand! He can't remember. He needs someone to find it for him!" Rumpel was red in the face; he was sweating.

"That is what I know, Rumpel. That is why I am staying here in Cold Rock to help him until the federal marshal comes."

"But how did you know about it, Slocum?" Rumpel was screaming. "How could you have known about it! That old man doesn't make any sense anymore. It was Dunroodie who knew about the gold. Dunroodie and Mae! Even I didn't know. That's why I got Dunroodie out of jail. How did you know? That old man can't even talk a straight sentence. How did you know!"

Slocum's grin was even more wicked than before. "I didn't, Rumpel. I didn't know."

Rumpel's furious red face had now turned the color of white ash. "You . . . didn't know? Then how . . . ?"

Slocum's voice was soft as a kitten now as he said, "You just told me, Rumpel. That's how. You just told me."

Hours later, as he lay with the girl in bed in his hotel room, he thought again how different she was from most of the women he had known. There was a simple innocence she had that excited him completely, and that he felt seeping into him more and more.

They spent most of the day in bed, only coming

out in the evening for some supper. He bought a bottle of champagne to celebrate the end of all of it.
"Let's drink to Hank Larrabee," he said.

"He's a lovely man. Can I ask you something?
What do you think it was he was talking about? I
mean that caused him all that terrible happening."

"I don't really know. But you know how those old
prospectors often are. They talk all the time—to
themselves, to the sky, to anyone within hearing distance. But most people think those fellers are crazy,
so they don't listen. I asked him what he was talking
about that set somebody on him, but he says he
doesn't remember. And I believe him. Also, he
might have figured out who Dunroodie was."

"Hmm." She smiled at him, holding her champagne glass to her lips. "How did you figure out who
Dunroodie was?"

"Me? I just wondered why he ever would leave a
woman like his wife. And when I saw him spend all
that time in the Lost Mine not looking at her, I figured there was something there. She *is* a beautiful
woman, after all."

"His wife?"

"Dunleary. Mae Dunleary. It's related to my
theory that when people change their names—some
people—they don't necessarily like to get rid of the
whole thing. See, he didn't have to play that game of
pretending to be looking for Dunroodie. He couldn't
resist it."

"You figured that she was Dunroodie's wife? That
man Roller's wife?"

"I took a wild guess. And she had to keep part of
her name too."

"So what will happen to her?"

"I don't know. Nothing, I suppose."

There was a slight reddening of her cheeks as she looked at him.

"What's the matter?" he asked.

"You said she was such a beautiful woman."

"You're jealous?"

"Yes, I am. You say she's beautiful, and I know I'm not. I'm ordinary."

"Well, see, I'm a little crazy, too. I happen to be like Old Hank. Talk to myself and all like that."

"So . . . ?"

"Well, the trouble is, I like ordinary women. You know the kind, dowdy, overweight, kind of dumb, too, and not much interested in physical fun."

"You beast! And what do you mean by physical fun? I never heard of that."

"See? That's just why I like dumb women like you who don't know what something is, say, like physical fun."

"Then, Mr. Slocum, I want you to teach me."

He grinned at her. "I'll think about it."

"You'll think about it! Indeed!"

"I've just thought about it."

"And . . ."

"And—and I want you."

JAKE LOGAN
TODAY'S HOTTEST ACTION WESTERN!

__SLOCUM AND THE HANGING TREE #115	0-425-10935-6/$2.95
__SLOCUM AND THE ABILENE SWINDLE #116	0-425-10984-4/$2.95
__BLOOD AT THE CROSSING #117	0-425-11233-0/$2.95
__SLOCUM AND THE BUFFALO HUNTERS #118	0-425-11056-7/$2.95
__SLOCUM AND THE PREACHER'S DAUGHTER #119	0-425-11194-6/$2.95
__SLOCUM AND THE GUNFIGHTER'S RETURN #120	0-425-11265-9/$2.95
__THE RAWHIDE BREED #121	0-425-11314-0/$2.95
__GOLD FEVER #122	0-425-11398-1/$2.95
__DEATH TRAP #123	0-425-11541-0/$2.95
__SLOCUM AND THE TONG WARRIORS #125	0-425-11589-5/$2.95
__SLOCUM AND THE OUTLAW'S TRAIL #126	0-425-11618-2/$2.95
__SLOCUM AND THE PLAINS MASSACRE #128	0-425-11693-X/$2.95
__SLOCUM AND THE IDAHO BREAKOUT #129	0-425-11748-0/$2.95
__STALKER'S MOON #130	0-425-11785-5/$2.95
__MEXICAN SILVER #131	0-42511838-X/$2.95
__SLOCUM'S DEBT #132	0-425-11882-7/$2.95
__SLOCUM AND THE CATTLE WAR #133	0-425-11919-X/$2.95
__COLORADO KILLERS #134	0-425-11971-8/$2.95
__RIDE TO VENGEANCE #135	0-425-12010-4/$2.95
__REVENGE OF THE GUNFIGHTER #136	0-425-12054-6/$2.95
__TEXAS TRAIL DRIVE #137	0-425-12098-8/$2.95
__THE WYOMING CATTLE WAR #138	0-425-12137-2/$2.95

Check book(s). Fill out coupon. Send to:

BERKLEY PUBLISHING GROUP
390 Murray Hill Pkwy., Dept. B
East Rutherford, NJ 07073

NAME_____

ADDRESS_____

CITY_____

STATE_____ ZIP_____

PLEASE ALLOW 6 WEEKS FOR DELIVERY.
PRICES ARE SUBJECT TO CHANGE
WITHOUT NOTICE.

POSTAGE AND HANDLING:
$1.00 for one book, 25¢ for each additional. Do not exceed $3.50.

BOOK TOTAL $_____

POSTAGE & HANDLING $_____

APPLICABLE SALES TAX $_____
(CA, NJ, NY, PA)

TOTAL AMOUNT DUE $_____

PAYABLE IN US FUNDS.
(No cash orders accepted.)

202b